MOSQUITO DRILL
A STORY CYCLE

BY JOHN MARMOT

Mosquito Drill

Copyright © 2010 by 302 Publishing

All rights reserved. Published in the United States by 302 Publishing, Portland, Oregon

No part of this book may be used or reproduced in any manner whatsoever without written permission except in the case of brief quotations embodied in critical articles or reviews.

The characters and events in this book are ficticious. Any similarity to real persons, living or dead, is coincidental and not intended by the author.

Publisher's Cataloging-in-Publication
(Provided by Quality Books, Inc.)

Marmot, John.
    Mosquito drill : a story cycle / by John Marmot.
    p. cm.
    LCCN: 2010904755
    ISBN-13: 978-0-9790165-0-9
    ISBN-10: 0-9790165-0-9

    1. Convenience stores--Fiction. 2. Employees--Fiction. 3. Self-reliance--Fiction. 4. Control (Psychology)--Fiction. 5. Northwest, Pacific--Fiction. I. Title.

PS3613.A7668M67 2010   813'.6
                                   QBI10-600077

Edited by Merridawn Duckler
Interior and Cover Design by Kyle Richardson, Enrich Design
Special thanks to Daniel Kimbro and Gabriel Edge

Find out more at www.302publishing.com

Most boys have seasons of wishing they could die gloriously instead of just being grocery clerks and going on with their humdrum lives.

Sherwood Anderson
Winesburg, Ohio

"I'll own up: I think it is a dream, Miss Verena. But a man who doesn't dream is like a man who doesn't sweat: he stores up a lot of poison."

Truman Capote
The Grass Harp

This is fiction.

CONTENTS

NIGHTSHADE

Smack Whore
11

Health and Beauty Aids
23

Cart Run
35

Cheese Island
51

MORNING GLORY

Tuesdays
71

Schadenfreude
87

Mosquito Drill
103

Beat Sunset
127

NIGHTSHADE

SMACK WHORE

We didn't know anything about her, not even her name. In all honesty none of us cared. Based on those bruised arms and squirrelly eyes of hers, not to mention the number of dolts she shopped with on a weekly basis, we figured she had to be some kind of drug addict – and not the least bit skanky.

It was game night at the store, one hour before Sunset, when the smack whore bent forward to watch me weigh her head of cabbage. Her two-tone shoulder-length hair, wet and matted from a recent shower, smelled sweet – like a honeydew melon. And she was bra-less under the same pink tank-top she'd worn the previous night.

"Hey there, baby darling," she said to draw my eyes. Her thin smile couldn't hide the perspiration dotting her upper lip. "Those girls are out biting in this heat, wouldn't you say?"

Behind the check-stand my knees buckled at the hard wink she gave. What were the chances I had misheard what she had said? The store was busy, noisy. We had five registers running, each with a line of customers stretching down an aisle.

"I beg your pardon?"

Her nose wrinkled. She dropped one finger over the counter and said, "That's one helluva mosquito bite you got there, *Dale*."

I looked to where she was pointing and she was right: there was a full-blown welt, the size of a dime, between my thumb and forefinger. I hadn't known it was there, didn't feel the bite whenever it'd happened.

The smack whore waited for me to hit the sub-total before reading the instructions on the remote panel in front of her. Then, sliding her food card, she went on to say that the girl mosquitoes need the blood for their eggs. "Can't lay the eggs without a little human blood. Try remembering that the next time you kill one of those suckers. Might make you think twice. About us girls, that is."

The cash drawer popped open. I ripped the receipt off the register and stuffed it in the plastic bag. She grabbed at the handles, ready to go, but stopped when she noticed the playing schedule taped to the countertop.

"Big game tonight," she realized.

"Yeah, it's my boss's daughter's team. I have complimentary tickets if you want…"

"Tickets? Are they free?"

I nodded. "Starts in an hour."

The clock on the wall struck six and she looked back from it, chewing on her lower lip. "What the heck," she said. "I'll take one, thanks for asking."

I opened a drawer and peeled a ticket from one of the stacks Tom had put in every check-stand.

She smiled at the ticket, her spontaneity, the whole idea of her going. "It might be fun. I haven't been to a game in years."

The smack whore pulled the grocery bag off the counter and started for the automatic doors, studying both sides of the paper ticket as she walked.

¢¢¢

Last week my store director, Tom Barren, had her inside the PIC office with the door closed. I could see them both talking through the little glass window. The impromptu meeting went on and on… They'd been in there so long that he feigned exhaustion when he finally got out.

"Smack whore," he said after she'd left the office. He stood in the doorway and watched her take a shopping cart down the beer and chip aisle. "Didn't think she would ever shut her trap."

"What'd she want?" I asked.

Tom flashed the job application he was holding. "What everybody seems to want these days – waste my time."

He tossed the application on the nearest desk and slapped me on the shoulder. "At least you're here. Let me show you something before I forget."

Moving purposefully across the main floor, my store director led me to the walk-in freezer in the backroom. *Carefree Highway* by Gordon Lightfoot was playing on the Muzak. In the frosty air he pointed to a ripped bag of frozen taters that had spilled across the floor, and said, "Nobody cares." Then he looked at me.

I agreed but said nothing.

The veteran grocery man shook his head as he continued surveying the cluttered freezer, hope fading fast with the milky haze. He closed the door behind us so that the fans would kick on, and they all did except for the one on the end. So he pulled off one of his black sneakers and whacked the protective cage overhead. Shards of ice flew across the room as the fan's blade whirred to life. I looked down to guard my eyes, only to notice a giant hole in the heel of my boss's thin black sock.

"Anyway," Tom said, "try and get this mess cleaned up if you can, or have one of the other guys, I don't care. I'm ducking out early tonight. Traci could use a little practice at the plate."

Traci, his daughter, played softball. Supposedly she was pretty good. Tom had high hopes of her making the next Olympics. She was only sixteen.

"They got Sunset on deck," he said with a shiver.

"Sunset's not going to be like Lincoln."

Whatever this meant. But him mentioning high school did remind me of Darby, my main closing courtesy clerk who was thinking about dropping out at the end of this, his junior year. I asked Tom if he had found time to sit down with him yet.

"Not yet," said Tom. "I'll try to get to it by the end of the week."

I stepped forward. "He just needs a little more money. Maybe we should train him to be a checker. That way he doesn't have to get two jobs and he can still go to school."

"What's that?"

"I said maybe we should train Darby to be a checker."

"Did someone just call my name?"

"Huh?"

"The intercom's broken in here," Tom said. "Did someone just call my name?"

I opened the freezer door and the fans automatically shut off. Tom slipped on his shoe, covering that giant hole in his sock, and went to the intercom on the backroom wall.

"Erin, intercom please, Erin!" His voice reverberated across the entire store. He let go of the speaker button and Erin, the store's head checker, picked up on the other end. He asked her if someone had just called his name and she told him that she wasn't sure, so he hung up the phone and waited a long second to hear if anyone would try calling him again. No one did.

So I tried picking up where we had left off. "Maybe we should make Darby a checker, you know, give him a promotion instead of just a raise."

But Tom didn't answer. His eyes were scanning the pallets of overstock along the bay wall.

"It'd be in everybody's interest, Tom. He'll be burnt out in a month if he gets another job."

"Sure, sure," Tom said, but I could tell it had gone in one ear and out the other. His mind was on temporary lockdown, all dreams teetering on Sunset. He picked up a push broom that was lying on the floor and swung it like a baseball bat.

¢¢¢

Once the softball game got underway, business slowed and the night was quiet except for a spider that Victor, one of the produce clerks, had found in a banana box. The South American spider looked big and mean, hairy all over, and he had fangs that were almost as long as his two front legs. Victor decided to keep him in a glass jar with holes in the cap. By the time I saw him, Victor and my closing checker, Kwan, had already named him and tried feeding him bits of lettuce and a couple of dead flies they had found under the plastic wrap machine. But their new pet, who they'd named 'Tom', showed no interest.

Kwan bet that it was because the things they had put in the jar weren't living anymore. That's when I offered up the Band-Aid I'd been wearing over the mosquito bite on my hand. All night I'd been scratching at it, not because it itched but because it was there, and when it started to bleed I went to the first-aid kit behind the customer service counter to get a Band-Aid. But the kit was close to empty (people get cuts in grocery stores all the time); there were no good Band-Aids to choose from. The one I ended up wearing didn't fit quite right, so it was easy to give up for the sake of science.

We all hovered around the glass jar, anticipating. Victor had me wrap the Band-Aid on the end of a long plastic straw that they were calling a 'feeding stick.' Then he pushed it through one of the holes and scraped it off at the bottom of the jar. We couldn't wait to see what the spider would do next. Kwan, at first, was sure the spider could smell my blood, but there really was no evidence of that. The spider, or Tom, just sat there. Like all he needed was a desk. Then Kwan wondered out loud if spiders hunt only at night. None of us knew the answer so we all went into the produce cooler that was pitch black when the lights were off. We stood in the dark for a minute, not a word spoken. Then we went back out to see if anything had happened. Nothing had happened. So we kept brainstorming ideas until the time came that we HAD to get back to work. We left it with Kwan saying he would bring in a live grasshopper tomorrow. We all smiled and nodded at this. Like it was something to look forward to.

¢¢¢

The smack whore dropped by after the game. She was wearing a green sweatshirt and jeans, not her usual late-night ensemble, and had a fighting bobcat painted beneath her left eye. Spotting me at the front of the store, she grabbed a hand basket and skipped alongside the row of check-stands.
"What a knuckle-biter!" she shouted. "Those girls played their brains out. And the crowd, you should've seen how many people there were. So much tension, the energy – it was unlike anything I've ever felt!"
"So you did go?"
"Damn right I went. And I'll be going to the next game too, you can count on that."
She skipped and twirled at the thought, amazed by the overall experience, then snuck through one of the closed check-stands and headed down the frozen aisle.
It was forty minutes before midnight – closing time – and there were no other customers inside the store. Kwan was on his last break and I was in his check-stand reading magazines, killing time until the clock behind the customer service counter said I

could start making the closing announcements.

I pulled out the stack of tickets and was studying them when the smack whore reappeared out of nowhere with a basket full of groceries. She unloaded each item onto the conveyor belt and put the basket on the floor. Her hair was pulled back into a ponytail and her face was flush from being in the night-air.

"I was sitting next to a single mother whose daughter plays for the other team. She says in the summertime they travel all over the country because of softball. Said they sold their house and rent an apartment so that nothing can stand in their way. Now that's dedication. Can you imagine?"

I couldn't. She paid cash for two frozen dinners, a bag of russet potatoes, and a pink energy drink.

"Who won the game?" I said.

The smack whore's shoulders dropped. "We lost."

"Against Sunset?"

"Yeah," she said, "against Sunset."

We both looked toward the doors that weren't moving for the time being. It was dark out and the sky was clear. She had a sweet smell that lingered in the store's heavy air; *Speedball Tucker* by Jim Croce was playing on the Muzak.

"What do you got there?" she said, looking over my shoulder at the glass jar sitting on top of the register. "Some kind of animal?"

I grabbed the jar and held it up so she could see. "It's a spider we found in a banana box shipped from Brazil."

She took the jar from my hand, studied the spider curled up under a lettuce leaf. "He's beautiful," she said. "A giant house spider."

"House spider? Are you sure?"

"Trust me," she said. "I used to teach science."

Gently she shook the jar so that she could show me its hairy abdomen. Then she untwisted the cap and set the jar down on the counter, hovering over the opening and peering inside.

"They're not considered aggressive. But he will bite you if he's scared."

Carefully she stuck in her hand. She tried coaxing the spider into moving. Drooped over the glass jar, her green arm looked like a stem wilting in a vase without water. Beauty captured, beauty released – she pulled out her fist and let her fingers bloom.

¢¢¢

"Smack whore," Kwan said when he got back from his last break. "I could see you and your girlfriend talking from the window upstairs."

We swapped places, Kwan went behind the check-stand and I headed upstairs. The bottom file drawer in Tom's office was where he kept all the current submissions.

Already the store had received over fifty applications for the month, most being from high-schoolers looking for a summer job. The remainder consisted of three men and seven women. Of the seven women, there was only one who claimed a teaching position in her list of previous work experience. The application said her name was Faye Hendrickson.

At the bottom of the page she referenced the phone number of an elementary school in Kentucky. She had listed only the school's name. On a whim I tried the number, figuring no one would be there this late anyway, but just to see if the place really did exist.

A man answered on the other end. "Yello."

"I'm sorry, is this Madison Elementary?"

"In the flesh."

"I'm calling about Faye Hendrickson. She used to teach there a few years back?"

Twelve o'clock here meant three in the morning there. I could hear the man sit down in a chair and close a desk drawer. Something heavy fell on the ground and he grunted when picking it up.

"Faye Hendrickson," the man repeated. "My goodness, there's a blast from the past. Sweet lil' Faye Hendrickson. How the hell is she doing?"

HEALTH AND BEAUTY AIDS

"DARBY STINKS," Tom shouted over the baler's running motor. Its hydraulic ram dropped to the point of impact, mashing then flattening the boxes inside, before lifting back up and screeching to a halt. I opened the safety gate and the old store director handed me another box from the pile on the floor. Nobody else was in the backroom.

"He has a smell problem," he said. "Erin was just in my office and said she can't work with him anymore. He was bagging a customer's groceries and his stench nearly brought her to tears."

Already I didn't like where this was going. I grabbed a few more boxes and stuffed them through the opening. "Why are you telling me this?"

"Because you're his friend. You know the kid better than anybody."

"We just work together," I said. "We're not that close." I shut the safety gate and pushed the button. Again the motor turned on and the ram started down.

Tom paced back and forth, deliberating, until the baler stopped. "You have to talk to him, Dale. He smells like a cruddy hamster cage."

"What do you want me to say? I don't have any experience with this kind of thing. I'm just the night manager."

"It's been a problem for too long," Tom said. "Doggone it, we're a grocery store. Customer service is our bread and butter."

"You're not answering my question."

"Heck, I dunno. Tell him to take a shower. Toss him a bar of soap. I don't care what you do so long as he freshens up."

I shook my head and Tom could tell he wasn't getting anywhere. So he dug into his vest pocket and pulled out a small green box. Inside was a plastic squirt bottle.

"Aftershave?"

"Straight from the HABA aisle. You can charge it to the store's main account."

"Seriously?"

Tom handed it to me and tossed the empty box inside the baler. "This has to stop," he said. "He treats me like his mother. Last week I had to tell him to get a haircut. Two weeks before that I gave him money to buy a new pair of slacks. And have you seen him today? He hasn't done either one."

Tom kicked at the pile of cardboard, sending an empty box clear across the room. With a pained expression stuck to his face, he rubbed his forehead with the heel of his hand.

"Bottom line is I got a new kid out there looking for more hours. I've got every reason to put him on the back wall and Darby in the bottle room."

"You can't do that. Darby needs the hours."

"No? What choice do I have? When your head checker can't ask for a carryout for fear of gagging, what other option is on the table?"

He had a point.

"Fine," I said. "Just give me a couple days before you make any changes to the schedule."

Thinking, dry-cursing to himself, the ex-marine paced back and forth until one of the checkers called him over the intercom to the front of the store. He left and I shut the safety gate, punched the start button. The ram dropped down and crushed.

¢¢¢

The new courtesy clerk is standing at the end of a check-stand, looking bored with nothing to do. His spiky blonde hair has been styled and gelled, his clothes are crisp with a sharp crease running down each pant leg. The other day he told me his name but already I've forgotten it, and he doesn't have a nametag yet. When I ask him to help me face the store, he scrunches his nose and forces a smile – like he doesn't understand.

"Facing," I tell him, "is grocery lingo for pushing product forward to give the impression that a shelf is full. We do it every Monday, Thursday, and Sunday. It's one of those stupid jobs that has to get done. Because they say people buy more stuff in a store that looks good."

Still the kid looks confused. So I take him down the soup aisle to show him exactly what I mean. I pull a few cans forward and then have him face a shelf by himself so he can get the general idea and I can make sure he's doing it right.

"The concept looks simple," I say, "but you'd be surprised at how many people around here can't do the easiest jobs."

"I can imagine," he says back.

We keep going and all the while he seems nervous, overly cautious so as not to appear incompetent. At this pace it would take him a year to finish the entire store. To calm him down I start telling him about all the mistakes I'd made when I first got into the grocery business. I tell him about how I couldn't see the difference between a leek and a green onion. I tell him about all the customer complaints I got from bagging groceries, and about the time I broke a customer's red wine bottle in the trunk of her Mercedes. I tell him every embarrassing moment that comes to mind and when we move to the next aisle I notice he's still moving slowly with that concerned look on his face.

"Listen," I say. "You need to relax. This isn't rocket science. Common sense will take you wherever you need to go."

I watch him pull a box of pudding forward, straighten it, then step back to check his own work.

"You don't understand," he says. "You don't have to teach me anything. Soccer tryouts are in six weeks. I'll be gone in a month."

The teenager kneels down and starts fixing a row of canned milk. He faces the entire shelf, labels out, before glancing back at me.

"She must've been pissed at you," he says.

"Who?"

"The rich lady about the red wine in her trunk."

She was. The car was brand new, jet black with a camel interior. Her husband dropped off the cleaning bill. It cost me three paychecks to get the stain out.

¢¢¢

I was halfway done facing the store when Darby came shuffling up the breakfast aisle. It was the first time I'd seen my closing courtesy clerk all afternoon. He looked disoriented, clutching the back of his neck as he staggered toward me, chalk-faced and pigeon-footed. Without warning he made a sharp turn and drove his body into the wall of cereal I'd just finished facing. Boxes went everywhere. He stumbled backwards, taking a hard spill across the white tiled floor.

"Jesus, Darby…"

The bewildered teenager blinked open his eyes, sat up on his elbows. Sweat dribbled down his ears, his hair a black mess. Up close he smelled foul – worse than ever – like burnt road-kill. I reached down to help him to his feet.

"I think I'm gonna throw up," he said.

"What???"

A switch went off and a surge of adrenaline shot through my body. In a moment of superhuman strength I threw him into an abandoned shopping cart and drove it like a dogsled to the bathroom on the other side of the store. I kicked open the door and dragged him straight to the sink.

What followed were two solid minutes of vocalized retching. Customers hoping to use the bathroom were pulling U-turns halfway down the hall. Over the sink counter he emptied his stomach and continued dry-heaving – until at last he was able to catch his breath, both of us grimacing in the puke-speckled mirror.

"I slipped," he said with a string of drool hanging from his mouth. "And the dairy case shocked me."

He lifted his right foot to show me the burn hole in the heel of his black sneaker. I bent down for a closer look. The hole was bigger than a quarter.

"That was no shock," I insisted. "Darby, you were

electrocuted."

Steam rose from the sink and clouded the oversized mirror as both of us shook our heads in amazement – though likely for different reasons. Darby was the unluckiest person I had ever met. Bar none. In his three years at the store he had been hit twice in the parking lot, bitten once by a dog through an open car window, had three fingers broken by baling wire and got a staph infection after dipping his arm into the lobster tank.

Each incident had its own file.

I shut off the faucet and sent Darby to the couch in the break room. Then I went back to the dairy section, where my initial suspicions of what had happened were easily confirmed.

There was a water leak in front of the milk case that had been around for almost a year, a plumbing problem Tom had refused to pay for and instead expected his courtesy clerks to mop up all the time. It was a constant mess. Every couple of hours a puddle the size of a small pond would gather along the back aisle, through which customers would step and wheel their carts, often leaving tracks around the entire store. Customers and employees voiced their complaints, yet the old store director held firm. Not until an old lady slipped and threatened to sue the store did he realize the extent of the problem.

The next day he brought in a shop vacuum.

His idea was simple: Snake a thirty-foot extension

cord from an outlet in the backroom to the dairy case on the main floor. Plug in the vacuum and a job that once required twenty minutes of blistering mop-work would be reduced, with the push of a button, to a high-powered albeit noisy thirty-second fix. Problem solved, pennies saved – for Tom it was the best of both worlds.

Now whoever had used the extension cord last had left it plugged in and sitting where the puddle would eventually be. So, naturally, when Darby slipped while stocking the milk, thus grabbing the lip of the metal case to break his fall, a surge of electricity shot through his body, big enough to trigger the store's backup generator.

Case closed. I unplugged the extension cord and went in search of a mop bucket. In the produce area's cutting room I found one on the floor, next to Darby, who was clutching his face and screaming in pain.

"Help me! My eye! It's burning!"

The smell of spilt bleach soaked the air. An empty mop bucket lay tipped on the floor. Quickly I pulled Darby's head under the sink's faucet and switched on the eyewash applicator.

"You're so fucking stupid," I shouted over the spray of water. "Why didn't you just listen to me and stay upstairs? Huh? Do I have to babysit you? Is that everybody's job around here? To babysit you?"

"I'm sorry," Darby kept saying. "I'm so sorry…"

Water continued shooting through the applicator and into his eye, across his nose and mouth – like one of those carnival water guns taking dead aim at the center of a painted clown's face. After a few minutes his whole head and half his body were sopping wet. I shut off the water and there he stood, shoulders trembling, nose dripping, humiliated and staring at the floor.

"Show me your eye," I said.

"Don't worry, I'll be fine."

"Open your goddamn eye!"

He stretched down his eyelid. I couldn't tell if the white part looked more irritated than inflamed.

"How does it feel?" I said.

Sniveling, he wiped his face with his apron.

"You don't need to see a doctor?"

"Uh-uh."

"I don't need to send you home?"

Again he shook his head, blinked both eyes.

"Dammit Darby, you can't keep being this unlucky. You need to make a change, get control of your life."

"Control?"

"You know, stop goofing around so much. Clean up your act, get a haircut. Buy some new clothes. Maybe put on some aftershave."

"Aftershave?"

He looked eager for direction.

"Listen," I said. "Don't take it the wrong way.

I'm telling you this as a friend. You need to work harder, you know, up your game. That new kid's been showing serious potential."

¢¢¢

Darby stuck around after the store closed to help me finish facing. By now his eye looked better and his feet weren't dragging so much. He had just started facing the cracker aisle when I went upstairs to run the reports. Ten minutes later he was on the HABA aisle with a cloud of scented aerosol floating over his head.

"Look what I found," he said to me with a balled-up fist. He uncurled his fingers. Resting flat in his palm was a gold wedding band.

"Where'd you find it?" I said.

Darby pointed down the aisle. "On top of a box of woman's hair dye. You think someone left it there on purpose? You know, like the glock?"

The glock… He was talking about the gun our grocery manager, Carlos, had found with the margarita mixers a few years back. Turned out a seventeen-year-old kid had dumped it on the shelf after robbing a restaurant down the street. It was a big deal. Carlos got on TV and for a few days the store was in the spotlight.

I took the ring, examined it… Fourteen karats, no engravings, meant for a man's hand and weighing more than a marble… I flipped it in the air, caught it, then turned for the PIC office.

"Wait." Darby raced ahead of me. "If nobody claims it, then it belongs to me, right?"

"What do you need a wedding ring for?"

I kept walking. It was getting late and we still had three aisles to face. Darby followed me to the service center where the store's Lost & Found was kept. I grabbed an envelope, sealed the ring inside. On the front I wrote 'HABA AISLE' with a permanent marker.

Darby sat up on the counter.

"I'll never get married," he said. "Not ever."

I opened the cabinet, pulled out the collection box. Every day it seemed personal items were being lost or abandoned. Uncapped on the counter next to Darby was the permanent marker. He picked it up and drew a black line around his finger.

CART RUN

P. LEVEN ANDERSON wouldn't like hearing this, but lately I've been having a recurring dream of him pulling the trigger on C-235. Never once have we talked about it, so every aspect of the dream is fake, except for him taking aim and shooting that sea lion dead. That really did happen. According to his friend, Sitting Cow, Leven had served nine months in prison for this inhumane act, during which time he had the animal's tag tattooed on the inside of his forearm – as proof, dare anyone ask.

Earlier in the week, while standing at the foot of my bed, the old man had roused me with a hard belch, hand outstretched, ink-faded remnants of C-235 reading upside-down. His eyes were red and knife-like under a pressed brow that funneled down his twice-broken nose. In a manner neither rushed nor slurred he snapped two fingers and said, "Fork over the keys."

"Huh?"

"I need the truck."

"For what?" I sat up, blinking at him. My roommate was in rare form, both sober *and* alert, wearing one of my red employee jackets scrunched to the elbows and a pair of fingerless biker gloves.

"Tom got word there's a shit-load of shopping carts at a house down the street. Wants me to go pick them up."

"Right now?"

"Yes, right now, goddammit!"

"But I got a dentist appointment at one o'clock."

"That's perfect," he said. "I could use the help."

He disappeared and slowly I got dressed. I stepped into the hallway and found him in the bathroom patting down his white hair with some water from the sink. You could tell he was treating this job very seriously. Like it was his last chance at looking respectable.

¢¢¢

Leven's closest friend was Sitting Cow, a three hundred pound middle-aged unemployable white man, whose real name was Brad. The two loiterers had gotten to know one another while hanging around the coffee counter in the deli department. For years they had been refilling their cups free of charge and found power in numbers whenever Tom came hollering for his extra nickels. Sitting Cow was the one who talked me into making Leven my roommate. Once when he was sitting alone at one of the little round tables, taking in his last cup of caffeine before calling it a night, he grabbed my arm as I was heading for the break room upstairs.

"Just heard about Melinda," he said into his cup. I stopped. "Damn shame. She was my favorite-looking deli girl."

This happened a few months earlier, just weeks before he was diagnosed with throat cancer, before the surgery that would force him to use a mechanical larynx.

"She'll be back," I replied. "You watch."

Sitting Cow got up from the table and tossed his coffee cup in the trash. Then he pulled out a pack of menthols and nodded toward the automatic doors. "Got a second?"

Outside, under the covered awning, Sitting Cow puffed on a cigarette. It was raining and the gutters were clogged. Streams of water spilled like jail bars in front of the store's main entrance.

"I have a favor to ask," he said, gently pinching the lit cigarette in the corner of his mouth. "Don't mean to take advantage of a man's hurt. Just can't see any way round it, I hope you understand."

"About Melinda?"

"Well, sort of." Sitting Cow rocked back on his heels and scratched at his throat. His gray flannel shirt had a plastic box of darts in the front pocket.

"Leven's been parked on my couch for the last

three weeks – ever since getting booted for not paying his rent. Now Mother's calling him a house plant and Leven has to find somewhere else to live."

"You mean a roommate?" The thought hadn't crossed my mind. Our apartment was still under her name and on a month-to-month lease. Soon as a one-bedroom opened up in the complex, I had plans of moving out.

"I dunno. Wasn't he in jail?"

"That was a misunderstanding."

"For killing a sea lion?"

Sitting Cow exhaled, buried the cigarette in the bowl of kitty litter. "We've all had our ups and downs," he said. "Didn't you help Melinda fix her teeth? That tin grin must have cost you a pretty penny. A grocery man like yourself can't have that kind of cash lying round."

"I thought you said he doesn't have any money."

"Leven don't, but I do."

"And if Melinda comes back?"

"For what? A *retainer*?"

The automatic doors opened and a woman customer walked out of the store. Sitting Cow followed her with his eyes. She got in her car and turned on the headlights, forcing him to drop his focus.

"I could help a little," he said, tapping the box of darts in his shirt pocket. "Offer you a share of my winnings."

"How much?"

Sitting Cow cleared his throat, gave a pained swallow. "She's got about a hundred and eighty thousand miles on her. A bit bumpy in the turns but she'll get you where you need to go."

¢¢¢

I followed Leven out to the truck and he drove, steering us up Watson Road to a long graveled driveway at the end of a side street. The gate was open but nobody was around. Quietly Leven studied the coffee-colored house tucked under a pack of fir trees.

"What are we waiting for?" I said.

Thinking, Leven pinched his bottom lip. A bulging vein trickled down the middle of his forehead.

"Tom says she's a basket-case. A real horder and a bit of a loon. Not sure how she'll take to us sniffing around her property."

"But they're our carts."

"Don't matter," Leven said, "not to a nut-bag. We'll have to go in on foot. Race in and race out, it's the only way."

He cut the engine but didn't move. There were still some calculations running through his head.

"How many carts you think fit in back of this thing?"

"How many does she have?"
"Caller said nineteen."
"Nineteen? That's crazy…"
Leven nodded. "It's the mother lode, all right."

Ah, yes, the mother lode. Nineteen carts at two bucks a pop would be a winning haul for the Vietnam veteran. Bigger than his monthly scrap-metal run. Better than knife-sharpening for an entire weekend. Hell, not even Leven's mole trapping business had seen that kind of cash flow.

Both of us got out of the truck and crept up the graveled driveway, crouching real low so as not to be seen. A rickety wooden fence ran along the right side of the property, with the house stretching up the left. Dirty windows behind bent and broken screens showed no sign of anyone inside. It was a beautiful day. The sun crept through the trees and speckled the grounds with light. Wet grass all around stood high above the ankle; everything looked run down and overgrown.

"Holy buckets," Leven said when he turned the corner, getting his first look at the pileup. He peered back at me with wide eyes.

"This is an abuse of civility," he whispered, "the spoils of war."

Better yet, it was a shopping cart graveyard. Parked alongside the carport were baskets of every conceivable make and model. There were flip-downs and double-deckers, carts made of hard plastic and those designed for families with two or more infants, not to mention a few flatbeds from a hardware store that had gone out of business a few years back. And while most of them were ours and in pretty bad shape, rusted from years of sitting out in the rain, this lady's vast collection had broken county and state lines, stretching from Washougal to Wilsonville, from Gresham to Hillsboro and beyond.

Leven tightened his gloves, hiked up his pants. The two of us moved in without saying another word. Swiftly I went about gathering our own carts, those with the red handles, while scrutinizing and then ultimately leaving behind the ones that were too old or too broken to bother rescuing. Pure adrenaline rushed through my veins. Though all we were doing was retrieving what was rightfully ours, draped in the crisp morning air was an ominous feeling pushing me faster than normal. I had forgotten how good it feels to work outside.

After rounding up about ten salvageable carts, I turned to see how my partner was faring, only to realize he had fled from the recovery effort.

"Leven!" I barked, caught between a shout and a whisper. I spotted him wandering across the house's back yard. "What are you doing? Get back here and help me out!"

But he failed to answer, instead looking transfixed as he stood along the banks of a marsh that ran up against the house's unkempt yard.

"Damn you, Leven! She's gonna see us!"

I hurried over to check what was the matter, casting fleeting over-the-shoulder glances the entire way. The ground was clumpy and uneven; wet grass and giant molehills left my shoes and pants caked with mud.

"Leven, we gotta get out of here. You hear me? We're trespassing. She could arrest us on the spot."

I tried pulling him by the arm, but the old man remained steadfast, undeterred, staring instead at a large group of ducks that had congregated in the middle of the pond.

The tips of his shoes touched the water; a slight wind pushed his bangs across his forehead as he took both hands and clapped them together, startling a few nervous ducks into the air. Watching them fly and then coast beyond the treetops, he smiled up at the blue sky before muttering, "Pintails," under his breath.

"*Pintails?* Who cares about pintails? We gotta get out of here. We gotta get these carts out of here before, before –"

KaWHAAAM!

The remaining ducks jumped, splashed and flew at the sound of the rear patio door sliding open. I glanced over my left shoulder in time to see the old woman exiting the house in her bathrobe, pissed off and clutching a curtain rod with both hands.

"Oh no," I realized. "It's her..."

I had recognized her immediately. Her long stringy black hair and hunched posture allowed for no misidentification. Her name was Dorothy Whitaker. But those of us who worked at the store referred to her only by her coupon sorting technique:

"... Little Miss Rolodex."

Leven kept his back turned to the house, watching the ducks circle the pond, sweep across the trees and then land back where they had started. He had no idea of the problem customer standing just an aisle's distance away.

"What are you motherfuckers doing on my lawn? I see you sons of bitches! I have permits and I'm gonna call the Bureau on your ugly pink asses!"

I tightened my grip around Leven's elbow. Eyes dancing in every direction, I was mapping potential escape routes with the other hand. But she had us trapped. Confrontation was unavoidable. I let go of Leven and waved at her – like a crossing guard to an oncoming truck.

"We just want our carts back," I shouted meekly. Then I pointed to the store's logo stamped across Leven's back. "See, we're not bad people. Remember me? I'm your friend... Dale... from the store..."

But Little Miss Rolodex had no interest in the facts, real or distorted. Clearly she had issues, none of which could be resolved by our unexpected visit.

Hammering the curtain rod against a barbecue lid, she told us to scram. But, crazy as it sounds, I couldn't leave the carts behind. To me they looked like unfed horses, suffering from malnutrition.

I started to beg. "Please, Dorothy… you know me. I'm your favorite checker, remember? *Meats bagged separate… not too heavy, not too light…*"

"No, you're from the paper. Are you taking pictures of my babies again? Is that it? Where's your camera? I want that film, you asshole!"

I backed up, my heels sinking in the mud. "Please don't hurt me… don't make me go in the water. I'm from the store. I like your babies, I like all babies… I don't know what you're talking about…" I flinched. "I'm a good person, I swear I am…"

Dorothy just shook her head at this as she grabbed onto the railing and slowly, carefully, stepped down from the back deck. Then, traversing through the mud and sopped grass, she used her weapon as a temporary walking stick, huffing and puffing, nostrils flaring, ever clearer the impressive hairs streaming from her receding chin…

"You're right!" I shouted. "I'm wrong! I'm sorry! I should have known better! Please, Dorothy. Listen to me, I'm begging you…"

But there was no stopping her. With each closing step she whipped that curtain rod toward me – like a piñata stick. I had no choice but to drop and curl into the fetal position. Cowering with my head buried in both arms, I whimpered for mercy – for understanding – when out of nowhere Leven shouted my name across the yard. He told me to quit being a pussy and to give him a hand.

Little Miss Rolodex stopped and turned her head toward Leven who, with both legs posted to the ground, was trying to muscle a long line of shopping carts up the graveled driveway. Clenched jaw, veins bulging in his neck and forehead, the old man was giving it his all but slowing down fast. Some of the cart wheels were digging deep into the gravel and getting all twisted and bent out of whack.

"I know you," she seethed at Leven, redirecting her rage. "You're the mole killer. Pipe bombs and pistol shooting, eh? You think that's how we do business around here?"

She stepped forward and Leven hunkered down. He dodged and winced at her threatening jabs while, to his credit, keeping both hands firmly affixed to the handle of the lead shopping cart.

"You're nuts, lady! *Mole killer?* What mole killer? Tell her, Dale! Tell her how I've never killed a goddamn thing in my life!"

"Don't you lie to me!" Now she was blocking his exit, taking wild axe-like swings at the shopping carts, all in an effort to get at his clamped fingers. BAM!
BAM!
"MOLE KILLER! MOLE KILLER!"

"Sweet Jesus, Dale! She's goin for the fingers!"

Desperation clung to Leven's voice. He told me to quit standing around and to do something, so I went in search of a rock. The plan wasn't to hurt the old lady, only to scare the curtain rod out of her hand. But in my meager attempt at finding a stone big enough for the job, my eyes happened to drift past the rear patio door that Little Miss Rolodex had left cracked open by mistake.

I'd never seen anything like it. Little rodents – wild vermin – had piled themselves high behind the door in a mosh pit of hyper-aggression. What were they? Rabbits? Rats? Dear God, could they be something in between? Whatever they were, the furry little hybrids were bull-rushing the glass, digging and burrowing, in a frantic stab at widening that crack in the door. They scraped and squeezed; they hopped on each other's backs… but it was their selfless teamwork, above all else, that commanded my support and respect.

"Hurry up," Leven cried out. "She's all cranked up!"

I raced across the patio, grabbed the door handle and pointed to them happily. "Hey Dorothy! You better mind these bunny-rats! You left your door wide open!"

Dorothy turned back to the house and let out a horrified scream. But before she could get there in time, I'd widened the door an inch and the dam of rodents had broken free.

The little critters scattered across the backyard, scrambling behind trees and under hedges, without question running for their lives. What a liberating sight to behold! I was rooting for them so hard that I nearly forgot the reason I was standing there in the first place.

Then Leven shouted my name as the old lady barreled towards me. Turning, we raced in opposite directions – Little Miss Rolodex toward her beloved babies and me toward my prized shopping carts.

Leven made room for me on the handle, one that was already slick from his own sweat. Together we shoved the lead shopping cart with all our weight. The long line of welded metal, first squirming then contracting like a molting snake, eventually gave way to our shared determination. The wheels broke free and the long line of carts sailed forward. Soon we managed to reach the blacktop, tired and out-of-breath.

Not every cart could fit in the bed of the truck, so we hid the rest in a ditch for later. It was a little past noon. Leven started the engine and I rolled down my window. The vinyl seats were hot from the sun.

¢¢¢

Three additional trips were needed to get all the shopping carts out of the ditch. Afterwards, Leven offered to drive me straight to the dentist from the store.

Going to the dentist wasn't my idea. But since I hadn't been in so many years, and because the store had recently changed to a provider who required annual checkups for full coverage, I had to go and fill out a bunch of forms in the waiting room before I could finally get in a chair. They were tedious forms, asking questions that not even I cared about. My eyes kept drifting to the fish aquarium on the table against the opposite wall.

"For what it's worth," Leven said, sitting next to me, "you probably shouldn't have done what you did – setting those chinchillas free. Those suckers breed like rabbits. They could upset the whole natural order of things."

"Huh?"

"Barn owls feed on squirrels. But now with them getting fat on chinchilla meat, the damn squirrel population is gonna skyrocket and nest in the branches which you know will only hurt the stinking trees. And once the trees go, you can forget about everything else. Oregon loses its green gold, unemployment spikes, and then every school in the goddamn state goes in the tank."

He stood up, limped over to the twenty-gallon tank filled with uninteresting fish and enough algae to make the water look green. Into the glass he said, "That's the problem these days. Nobody thinks about the consequences."

Consequences? You shot a sea lion, I wanted to remind him.

Leven glanced over his shoulder. The receptionist had her back to the glass partition and we were the only ones in the waiting room. He scrunched up his jacket sleeve and stuck his hand in the water. Swabbed a big gob of algae from the corner of the tank and held it out for me to see.

"Good god," he said. "What should this tell you? Probably the whole place is tainted. Think of the dirty pliers, the soiled drill bits…"

Algae dripped from his finger and onto the carpet as he walked over to the receptionist's counter and rapped on the glass. The woman working back there turned to him holding up his slimed finger, wet to the forearm, C-235 right-side-up but faded.

"You see this?" shouted Leven. "How do you think your customer feels? Devil's in the details! You hear me? Algae is like green plaque!"

The startled woman locked the window slide and hurried down the hall.

Leven sat back down in his chair, wiped his finger on his pant leg. He reached down and grabbed the back of his shin. "I'm getting too old for this," he groaned. "Lousy carts, think I pulled me a calf muscle."

CHEESE ISLAND

CARLOS MERCADO ALMOST FORGOT to tell me about the kid who died. The two of us were sitting in the PIC office, a few minutes before the start of my shift, when the refrigeration alarm next to the safe went off. My grocery manager, looking more irked than surprised, leaned back in his chair for the panel on the wall. He held down the reset key until the red light blinked and the chirping sound stopped.

"Damn cheese island," he said. "Keeps shutting down for some reason. I put in a call. Refrigeration guys should be out here any minute."

From my locker I grabbed a rolled-up apron that had been tossed in back. Wrinkles were everywhere. The dentist appointment had taken longer than expected and my good apron I'd left at home by accident, on the living room floor, under the couch.

"Either way," Carlos said, "tonight shouldn't be too busy. Business has been slow and the store looks dialed. Let's see…" He pored over the notepad on his desk. "Tom left for the hospital, we're out of the 5-pound sugar on sale in the weekly, and we still need to do something about that potato chip display up front…"

"What happened to Tom?"

"Oh, his daughter had softball practice last night and sprained her ankle or broke it or something. I swear the guy freaks if she gets a bruise. He's crazy to think she'll ever make the Olympics. You ever seen those girls? They're built out of brick."

Carlos kicked up his feet as he continued to digress, gradually shifting to his usual rant about how our store director was never around anymore. I stood in the doorway and watched customers drive their shopping carts through the store's main aisles. There's something soothing or spellbinding in the way they move under the fluorescent lights, seeping through the aisles so fluidly – like a milk spill across grouted tile. Add to it the colorful displays, the beeping registers, the constant swishing and swooshing of those main doors opening and closing… It's like watching a cold river tumble – you can feel the numbness roll through your body.

I turned back to Carlos who was reading a People magazine. The clock above his desk said my shift had already started. But in reaching for my timecard I felt temporarily paralyzed, overcome by the sudden need to ask a simple question.

"Carlos," I said. He glanced up at me from a

spread of Worst-Dressed Celebrities. "How do you put up with this shit every day?"

He just smirked, flipping through the pages. "Don't worry, you'll get there eventually. One day you'll realize nothing good ever comes from getting upset. Sucks up too much energy and wastes all your time." He paused, as if digesting his own advice. Then he chuckled. "What am I saying? You're a night manager – go find a hooker and buy her a drink."

"Right…"

"Which reminds me." He tossed the magazine aside and pulled a pen from his shirt pocket. "Liquor Control's on the prowl again. This morning they stung a gas station down the street. Guess there was a nasty accident on Watson last night. Bicyclist slammed into a pickup truck and Tom wants everybody on high alert."

"Last night?"

Carlos nodded. "Right at the corner of Watson and Oakley. Tom had to go around when he drove in this morning. Said it was a real mess. Thinks OLCC will be doing stings all over the place."

"So the driver was drunk?"

"Nope, the bicyclist."

"The bicyclist? And he's a minor?"

"He *was* a minor," Carlos corrected.

"You mean he died?"

"Last I heard." Carlos got up from his chair and

went to his jacket hanging on the wall. After putting it on he turned and pointed to his own nametag. His lips moved like he was asking me a question – but I couldn't hear what he was saying. The mere mention of an underage drinker sent my pulse rising, hammering inside my ears. It swallowed my focus, every thought flashing back to that kid who had gone through my line the previous night. What were the chances of it being the same one? What did the bicyclist look like? Did he have curly hair? An orange goatee? I needed more information but Carlos just stood there, looking at me with a blank expression, like he had nothing more to give.

"Dale?"

"Huh?"

Carlos pointed to my apron and repeated his question. "What happened to your nametag?"

My teeth were polished but my goddamn gums were killing me, all four wisdoms, the hygienist said, were impacted and needed to be taken out. I dropped one hand from my jaw to my chest, over a heart that was pounding in place of where a nametag would normally be, and then looked at Carlos who was waiting patiently for an explanation…

"It's gone."

"Gone? What do you mean it's gone?"

I took a breath, dropped both shoulders. The kid's receipt was gone, out with the trash.

My heartbeat slowed as Carlos started rummaging through a desk drawer. Searching feverishly, he dug through loose paperclips, pens and pencils, sign clips and rolls and rolls of strapping tape, checking every nook and cranny like finding me a nametag was now the most important thing in the world. Give it up, I wanted to tell him. What's wrong with you? People are dying all around us and you're worried about a fucking nametag?

It was pathetic.

Carlos slammed the bottom drawer and checked his watch. He said he had to go. His ex-wife was out of town so he had to pick up the kids. As for the nametag…

"I'll have to order you one tomorrow."

He headed out of the office just as the refrigeration alarm started chirping again. But this time, instead of stopping to address it, Carlos waved goodbye and said not to worry – "It's just the cheese island. The refrigeration guys should be out in a little bit."

¢¢¢

Shortly after Carlos leaves I realize the mistake I had made. The store's name, address and phone number are stamped across each of the grocery bags. If that dead kid had one of them on him at the time of the crash, maybe hanging from his bike handle or tucked inside his backpack, all the cops would have to do is question every checker working last night and at most request the backup receipt rolls from each register. What a boneheaded move I made! What was I thinking? I should never have given the kid a goddamn bag!

    Soon business picks up and we're swamped. I flail through every order at thirty-rings-per-minute until there's a gap long enough for me to switch off my light, rope off the check-stand. Over the intercom I ask every checker to pick up a handset. Look alive I tell them. Look alive because there could be a bumble bee in the house. Gas station down the street just got hit and Tom thinks Liquor Control's headed our way. Everybody listening? Lindsey? Carol? Kwan? Maddie Rae? Don't hang up. You need to listen to me. From now on I want you to card everybody. And I mean everybody. I don't care if they look sixteen or sixty. If they're buying beer or wine or anything alcoholic, you ask for identification – no ifs, ands, or buts. You check their birthdays, check the expiration dates, match the picture, match up their weight and height and hair color, make sure the card's not cracked or peeling or fake. Do everything by the book. And don't be afraid to use your gut. Don't sell if it doesn't feel right. An angry customer isn't worth losing your job over. Everybody got it? Nod to me if you got it. Good. There was an accident on Watson last night and this is no coincidence. They're looking to blame somebody. These motherfuckers smell blood on our hands.

¢¢¢

All night long I have my eyes peeled, watching those doors swishing and swooshing; I size up every customer walking inside. I watch how they behave, how they shop, since those OLCC operatives are such bastards to pick out. It's impossible to get any work done. Later I catch Lindsey selling beer without asking for identification. I pull her aside, threaten to cut her hours. You can tell she doesn't give a shit. As I walk away, across the front of the store, she flips me the bird and says, "Go build something."

¢¢¢

Carlos was right, Lindsey too. The potato chip display at the front of the soda aisle was starting to sag, tilt, and threaten the wellbeing of any innocent shopper strolling past. Evasion is never an option. Something had to be done.

I went to the backroom in search of a replacement. A thorough scan of the store's inventory uncovered a half-pallet of assorted pastas, thirty or so cases of spaghetti sauce, some swanky-looking olive oil and enough minced clams to feed Mussolini's army. Yes, building an end-base with an Italian theme looked to be my best option, but for the amount of work I was about to put into the project, I wanted to make sure that there was enough overstock to keep the display going for more than a few days. Don't get me wrong, the answer was there – I just wanted a little more. Tonight I needed this display to be beautiful.

Next I made the rounds. In the bakery I wanted to see what they could add to the display. They didn't have much. I stole from a pile of week-old French bread that was being saved for turning into croutons. In the floral department I asked if they had any wicker baskets to spare. The girl who was working back there gave me three, and when I told her that I was building a display with an Italian theme, she started talking about Venice and how she had always dreamed of one day taking a ride in one of those gondolas. Sometimes, she confessed, she would gaze across the store and imagine the aisles as mini-canals and the shopping carts as little boats floating past. She looked down, went back to trimming the ends off of roses. What could I say? Some days you make the best with what you got.

After pilfering four cases of white and two cases of red from the wine steward's bargain rack, I now had enough product to move forward. Dismantling the existing display was the easy part. The few remaining bags of chips all made it to the shelf, and with a gentle push, the tower of leftover cardboard crashed to the floor. The empty boxes I took to the backroom, smashing them flat in the baler before collecting five wooden pallets to use as a solid foundation for my newest creation. Across the main floor I wheeled the base with a pallet jack, then set a giant piece of plywood on top to act as the initial shelf. I craved making a statement, building a monster. Up went three more levels supported by empty milk crates. I stepped back for a better look, then added two more. Now the shell was complete and all that remained was for me to stock and decorate the display in a way that would be attractive to the passing eye.

The cases of spaghetti sauce I stadium-cut out front, hiding the wooden pallets from view. The minced clams I cut into trays and ran along both sides and across the middle shelf. Next came the pasta. There were four varieties: angel hair, spaghetti, penne rigate and lasagna noodles. I piled them all like log houses on every shelf, spotting the wine and the olive oil in between to act as stabilizers. Last I pulled out a ladder and positioned the two wicker baskets on the very top, decorating them with the loaves of French bread that were too old to sell. I stepped down and backed away. The display was beautiful, quite possibly the best one I had ever built… and still something was missing. It needed more color. So I returned to the floral department to ask another favor. Earlier I had caught glimpse of some budding daffodils…

¢¢¢

Customers stop throughout the night to admire the display. One calls me a craftsman, another an artist. I take each compliment in stride, busily straightening, adding whatever finishing touches, when – *Swish…* The doors break and in walk this guy and girl who catch my attention. I'm standing high on the ladder as they skate across the white-tiled floor, two lovebirds arm in arm. The girl is in her late teens, wearing a tank-top, jean skirt and a pair of beige boots lined with sheepskin. She has black hair, nice and curly, and pasty unmarked skin more sexy than sickly. Her soft blue eyes tell me she's sweet, honest, a young woman with a strong moral compass, none of which could excuse the cocksucker she's locked elbows with… He dares come into the store wearing a black hooded sweatshirt with the drawstrings pulled so tight that you can't see his face, not even his chin. He looks ready to rob the place, so I ask him to take off the hood if he wants to keep shopping in the store. I'm not rude about it, but I'm not exactly polite either. Why should I be? If common sense is so widespread in this world, how come I'm the asshole who always has to point it out?

Both stop and turn to face me. The girl's jaw tightens behind a pursed set of lips.

"What did you say?"

I step off the ladder to repeat myself, this time posing the request more as a statement of fact than as a question. I say: "Your friend needs to take off his hood if he wants to shop in this store." Then I point him out to her, just in case there's any confusion.

She crosses her arms and scowls at me. "Is this a fucking joke?"

She takes a step forward. Then, like a cherry bomb exploding in my face, she pops up and starts rattling off all the rights her man has – a real professor of the law – like she's just finished her civics course at the local community center down the street. She tells me that a retailer has no control over what a customer can or cannot wear, even citing a case in which NO SHOES, NO SHIRT, NO SERVICE did not hold up in a court of law. Also weaved into her argument are more colorful words that at best give me free liberty to tell her how full of shit she really is. Because – and not to shine my own apple – I do know a thing or two about who I can and cannot kick out of my own store. I know that I can't be racist or sexist. I know that I have to be ultra-careful of how I conduct myself for fear of getting my ass sued. Not that I am racist or sexist or guilty of anything more than a little profiling every once in a while. But what's so illegal about that? It's human nature. Who doesn't size people up on the first impression? Seriously. This bitch didn't know who she was talking to.

"We have a no hood policy," I tell her when she finally takes a breath. "If you or your man don't like it, you can take it up with the store director tomorrow. His name's Tom and he'll be here bright and early."

There's nothing more to add, so I grab the ladder and turn to walk away. And that's when I hear this squeaky little voice over my left shoulder. It says: "You don't understand."

It's him, the cocksucker. I swing back around and tell them both to get the hell out of my store. "Get the hell out or I'll call the cops." I completely snap. Hooded freaks, teenage drunk-driving bicyclists... Everyone wants to blame me for their problems and I'm sick of it. My hands are shaking so bad that I almost drop the ladder on my foot.

"You're an asshole," the girl says as they back out of the store. "Did you ever think that maybe my friend here has a disease? Did you ever think about that? Did you ever think that maybe he's really, really sick? Huh? Did you? I don't think so. You're too stupid to have those kinds of thoughts. You don't know anything. You think that everybody is the same. You think everybody reacts to everything in the exact same way. Well, let me let you in on a little secret, pal: PEOPLE ARE DIFFERENT." She says this last part really slow like I'm retarded or something.

"My friend has an illness," she shouts from outside the store. "If he gets too much sunlight, he could die. What do you think of that, Mister Manager? Huh? Huh?"

I stop short of the doors, reinforced by the sharp glow of the store's white light. Then I point up at the sky and remind her that it's night out. I say it real slow just to piss her off.

¢¢¢

By ten o'clock the refrigeration guys still hadn't shown up. Around the cheese island I touched the vents and the air was warm – but not that warm. I wasn't sure what to do. Pulling this much cheese to the back cooler would be a real pain in the ass. I picked up some Gouda, sniffed the plastic. How do you know when cheese goes bad? Blue cheese has mold, Limburger smells like shit…

I headed outside to wait. As I stepped out from under the glow of the fluorescent lights, the automatic doors closed behind me… *Sa-whoosh…* sealing off the constant swirl of recycled air and the melodic hum of Harry Nilsson or Cat Stevens or whoever was singing on the Muzak inside the store.

There's a soft breeze and not a single star outside the covered walkway. A thin layer of clouds crowd and cover a faint moon – like soapy water around a clogged drain. I unfold my arms, take a breath. The parking lot is littered with the usual run of late-night shoppers.

    I've held on to a lot of receipts over the years, just to cover my own ass. To keep my name from falling into the wrong hands. It's nothing new; the same old scene plays freely in my head: Blood everywhere… twisted limbs jutting through broken glass… and sitting on the passenger floor is the culprit, an open 12-pack, with a receipt tucked under its cardboard handle. The officer at the scene pulls the blood-speckled slip of paper and holds it into the light to read: DALE CATHER, CHECKER #171. Parents are notified. The Oregon Liquor Control Commission comes down hard. Lawsuits are filed. Fines are handed out. I lose my job, but that's the least of my worries. My reputation in the community has dropped to an all-time low, where surprise, surprise: not even a grocery store will hire me now. All because of a wise-ass kid set on pulling the wool over my eyes. As if I couldn't tell. As if my life wasn't shitty enough. No, sorry. I think I'd rather just sell you the beer and keep the receipt for myself. Skip that headache altogether. Because no receipt means no paper trail. Or more importantly, that it's your fuck-up and not mine.

    The warm night winds drench my skin; each breath I take seems to splash across the inside of my head. It feels relieving to know that whatever happens on the outside is someone else's problem. Still, I can't help but feel a bit uncomfortable, for the night is not yet over. Somewhere out there, in the darkness, lurks the sneaking suspicion that I'm about to get burned.

A car rolls past; headlights stream through my line of sight and force me to blink. Slowly I turn to a little girl standing behind the wall of a soda machine. She is young, maybe eleven, wearing a summer dress that looks as colorful as the detergent aisle. Her eyes are closed, a scratched violin flush against her chin. An open case lined in red velvet rests before her bare feet.

At first I can't hear what she's playing. My mind is still processing, too numb to register any of the noises around me. So as I stand there motionless, watching that bow scrape across the muted strings, my initial reaction is to feel sorry for her; no one this young should ever be begging for money. But, little by little, drop by drop, my ears gradually regain their function and the music pours in. Any compassion I have for this girl is fading fast. I am starting to feel envious of her god-given talent.

I can't tell what song she's playing or how long she's been standing there – just a handful of quarters lay scattered across the open case's plush red interior. But she looks comfortable and sounds well-practiced, never once opening her eyes to check her fingers along the finger board. She isn't just playing the music, she's being directed by it. With every high note rising then floating through the air, her body sways like a buoy to an ocean wave.

The song goes on for another minute, but not until she finishes the final note does she open her eyes to look at me. And when she does, she seems startled by my presence, nervously looking in every direction but forward. Whether she's hoping that I will make an exception or pretend that she isn't there, all I know is that her request is a simple one: night managers can be shamefully oblivious when they want to be.

"Where are your parents?" I say.

She shrugs and then shakes her head, like she doesn't speak a word of English.

"You didn't come here by yourself, did you?"

Again she doesn't answer, leaving me with little choice but to ponder the possibilities – on a night when all the possibilities seem imponderable.

"You know you shouldn't be out here alone," I say. "It might look safe, but you'd be surprised at what goes on around here. Bad stuff, crazy stuff…"

I search her eyes for some sort of reaction, but they remain in a fixed stare over my right shoulder. Then they light up and she nods slightly, causing me to turn to a van that is parked in one of the handicapped spots behind me. The engine is off and sitting in the front seats are a man and a woman who I take to be the girl's parents. They just smile and wave at me, more hopeful than nervous, more guilty than innocent.

I turn back to the little girl who's already packing up. No further explanations are necessary. The van's engine coughs to life, its rear door slides wide open. She gets in and I check my watch. Ten more minutes, I think to myself. I'll give the refrigeration guys ten more minutes.

MORNING GLORY

TUESDAYS

Tom wasn't being Tom on the day Zeus the Carpenter was scheduled to arrive. He was acting strange, running around the main floor like a chicken with his head cut off. Dusting shelves. Bagging groceries. Picking up baskets and barking out orders. It was Tuesday and he was still upset over his daughter's softball injury which had, as it turned out, proven to be more serious than originally expected. The knee specialist out in Woodburn had come back with news that was damning: she actually did tear her ACL. Now with Traci sidelined for the rest of the season, so were any hopes of her making the next Olympics. Everyone at work felt bad for the old store director. Even Victor, who rarely spoke unless spoken to, shared in Tom's disappointment. While reshaping a pile of blood oranges into a pyramid, the forty-year-old produce clerk said all dreams are perishable and come with expiration dates. Some days you're better off throwing them out than pushing them to the back of the shelf.

¢¢¢

Tuesday nights were never about the work; they were about the long gaps in between. There wasn't a freight load to worry about, we didn't have the entire store to face, and the overall number of customers shopping, for whatever reason, was always less than any other day. It was like there'd been a meeting and Tuesday had drawn the shortest straw. You'd think some people would catch on and shop on Tuesdays because no one else did. But this never happened, so for those of us who had to work, the inexplicable developed into a kind of rule. Tuesdays were ours. They belonged to us.

Every Tuesday Darby liked to spend his first break under the Keno monitor, watching the numbers fall. He'd compare the numbers on the screen to those on the lottery ticket he was holding, sometimes double-checking, triple-checking the results. Never once in our years of working together had I seen him win. Always he'd crumple that little slip of paper and toss it in the trash.

That afternoon I was loaning money to the deli register as he stood beneath the monitor. Eyes wide, full of hope, as random numbers went sprinkling down the screen, there appeared a subtle but noticeable difference in my closing courtesy clerk. He looked taller than usual.

"Cowboy boots, Darby?"

Flinching, the ratty teenager spun round on his two-inch heels, both arms folded tight across his chest. He looked nervous, borderline nauseous, as he pulled an employee handbook from his back pocket and opened it to the store's uniform policy. Evidently he'd spent all morning gearing up for this showdown.

"You're kicking the wrong mule," he said. "Manual says only black shoes. Nowhere does it say anything about not allowing boots."

"Yeah, but you can't run in those things, Darby."

We both looked down at his choice of footwear, at the fake black lizard-skin gleaming in the fluorescent light. Darby stretched his legs, widened his stance – in a flash he took off at a dead sprint, across the main lobby and down the soda aisle. It was the fastest I'd ever seen him run. CLOP-CLOP, CLOP-CLOP, CLOP-CLOP... Startled customers turned at the sound of his thunderous heels. They watched him pull up at the end of the aisle, slide, then reverse his direction. CLOP-CLOP, CLOP-CLOP, CLOP-CLOP... He raced back to where I was standing and skidded to a stop.

"I've checked all the forecasts," he said, hunched over and panting. "From here to Boise and there's nothing but clear skies for the rest of the week. Hey Zeus should be in our parking lot come nightfall, God willing."

"Hey Zeus?" I repeated.

Darby knelt down and refitted the cuffs of his workpants around his boot shafts. "He keeps count on a clicker for every time someone shouts 'Hey, Zeus!' to him from a passing car. By Pittsburgh he had three clicks, by Des Moines he had seven. It's the stupid media, I think. Hardly anybody knows he's out there."

Now I remembered. Some religious nut had been traveling with his donkey from a lighthouse in Maine, pushing a crucifix across the country in an effort to spread the word of Christ. The cabinet maker whose actual name was Zeus Mulroney, had been a practicing atheist up until the day he saw the reflection of a long-bearded man in the spinning blade of a rotary saw. His route had him passing the store on his way to the 99. Tom had mentioned it in our last employee meeting.

"I read in his web journal how Frosty likes parsley," Darby said. "Frosty's his sidekick. I was going to buy her a bunch for when they get here, but produce only has Italian in back. That shouldn't matter, should it? You think a donkey can tell the difference between regular and Italian?"

I shrugged. "It matters to people."

Right then Darby got called over the intercom for a price-check. His break was over and so was the lottery game, its final numbers blinking across the blue gridded screen. He crumpled his ticket, threw it in the trash, then moseyed toward the front of the store. At the deli register I was recording the loan when again the intercom bell rang, this time for customer service on the baking aisle.

An older woman looked up from the shelf's glaring hole when I rounded the corner. 5-pound sugar was on sale in the weekly and we'd been handing out rain-checks all afternoon. In her hand was one of our coupons.

"You guys are always out of something," she said.

Two aisles over I could hear Darby running. CLOP-CLOP, CLOP-CLOP, CLOP-CLOP… It sounded like he had a clear path to whatever price he was checking.

The woman cleared her throat, tightened her grip around the shopping cart. I offered her a rain-check which she rejected outright.

"Doesn't anybody care?" she said.

I scanned the shelves until I found a substitute for the sugar, a 10-pounder of the same make. At first she looked at me like I was crazy. But then she made room for it in her cart.

¢¢¢

Throughout the night Darby stood inside the sliding glass doors, waiting, watching the usual bustle out in the parking lot, while the rest of us did nothing but race Matchbox cars up and down the breakfast aisle. It was Kwan's idea. Earlier in the afternoon my closing checker had noticed one of the cereal brands was offering a toy car inside every box. But what made this promotion different from all the rest was if the car turned out to be a Porsche Turbo, then you would win an actual Porsche Turbo. A heck of a deal, the mere possibility thrilled us beyond words. Of course the odds weren't in our favor, but what the hell, Victor and I chipped in and the three of us bought a box anyway.

Kwan liked our chances. The college dropout turned on-line poker addict had reason to believe luck was on our side. But as we hurried to the backroom with the cereal box in hand, there came a sudden but appropriate realization: How could we possibly own a car three ways? I suggested we sell it and split the proceeds, but Victor said we'd have to do that over his dead body. Driving a Porsche, he said, was not a right but a privilege. That's all he had to say about that.

Proper ownership and every other detail we agreed to hash out later. For now, all eyes were on the cereal box I was holding. Tension hung in the air as Kwan and Victor, both jittery with anticipation, allowed me the honor of pulling out the winning car. I felt the responsibility of a surgeon, carefully opening the top and slicing the plastic bag with my box-cutter, before digging one hand deep inside to begin navigating my way through the colored marshmallows and sugary flakes. Kwan and Victor stood off to the side, recording my every move, anxious for any indication that their lives had been forever changed. Their minds, you could tell, were projecting forward to a bright and shiny future, one involving high speed, immense handling and open roads twisting through hills and mountainsides, across deserts and along streams, leading anywhere and everywhere, but most importantly, to no place in particular.

The strength of these images, however potent, only made things worse, as for the life of me I couldn't find a prize anywhere inside the bag. Kwan, alert to my growing fears, ripped the box out of my hand and shoved his own fist down into the bag. Pressed brow, pursed lips, he had the face of pure resolve. He checked every corner, every inch, just like I had, until at last he too came out empty-handed.

We were outraged. Victor took the box and poured all the cereal onto the floor. Then he ripped out the plastic bag and flung the box against the backroom wall. Every action was countered with a more extreme reaction: one of us would kick a garbage can, another would pull and smash a rotten melon across the floor. And so on. Our emotions, getting ever sharper, were liable to tear the whole place apart. Thankfully, before things got too out of hand, Kwan spotted the yellow vehicle resting in the corner. It must have skated out when we weren't looking. Victor went over and picked the car up. It wasn't a Porsche Turbo. It was a Chevy Impala.

An awkward hush fell across the room as each of us surveyed the mess we had just made. All around lied the remnants of hope squashed. Even more embarrassing was the realization of how much better life had been when we could call ourselves victims. It was like we had always known the dream was dead; now the only difference was we had no one left to blame.

Victor punched the swinging black door and stomped across the main floor, leaving Kwan and me to clean up his department. Neither of us cared enough to complain. A few minutes later, Victor returned with a shopping cart full of cereal boxes. When we asked him what he was doing, he pulled his produce knife from the leather sheath hanging off his belt and said, "Improving the odds."

He grabbed one of the boxes and cut an inconspicuous slit along the bottom edge, careful not to puncture the plastic inside. He shook the box, nudging the breach with his thumb, and out popped a red Ford Fiesta.

What a discovery! Those damn idiots at the cereal company had made a mistake: They put the prize outside the bag. Kwan and I were speechless, overwhelmed by Victor's never-before-tapped brilliance. Because of him our tanks of hope had been resupplied.

For the next twenty minutes, box by box, we pulled out every car. It was like Christmas – we took our time, we forced ourselves to appreciate every gift, even the bad ones. There were Ferraris and BMWs, Fords, Pontiacs and Chevrolets, pickups and convertibles, SUVs and utility trucks, a cop car, a security van, a news chopper on wheels... The last car had Kwan pumping his fist in the air and screaming in celebration before uncurling his fingers to read the unfortunate model name on the chassis. It was a black Acura Integra, circa 1992.

The three of us bowed our heads in frustration, random toy cars, smashed fruit and crunched sugared cereal resting at our feet. It was like a giant wave of misfortune had rolled in and rolled out, taking with it our hope, or even worse, our rage, and leaving us with useless scraps. Kwan called ourselves suckers, though in truth we were opportunists who had spent only four dollars. I tried pointing this out but it sounded pitiful. For almost a minute no one moved, nothing was said, until Victor, picking up one of the cars and studying it in the palm of his hand, cleared his throat and said, "We can't let this ruin our night."

¢¢¢

Whoever won, Victor explained, would get to keep every car in the lot. But first we had to select our teams. Kwan stuck to the classics, I snatched up most of the sports cars, while Victor seemed content with an odd assortment of all-terrain vehicles. On the breakfast aisle he quickly configured a system of races modeled from his experience as a slot-car racer, one weighted on fairness, honest play and, of course, sudden death.

At first the competition was fierce and fueled by each of our desires to win. Solid effort and natural ability were rewarded with high-fives. Rules were made up on the fly. Countless false starts and do-overs were tolerated in our aim for a definitive champion.

But then Darby showed up. He knew that it was too late for him to join in on the fun, so he stood off to the side, choosing instead to ponder the whereabouts of Hey Zeus, the missing crusader, who no one else seemed to care about.

"Maybe they found water," he said. "I read somewhere how donkeys hate water. They hate it. They fear it. They have to be trained. What if there was some kind of unforeseeable water obstacle – like a giant puddle on a bridge? What horrible, horrible luck that would be. Imagine a simple puddle resting between you and God."

Kwan, kneeling next to the taped starting line, tested the wheels of an orange Boss 302 Mustang. "That wouldn't be bad luck," he said, "just bad planning. Now everybody shut the fuck up so we can race."

The next round was sudden death. Moods shifted and smiles faded away. Victor, who earlier had been projected as the dark horse, pulled ahead in the rankings and took a sizeable lead, as our classic and sporty cars proved no match to the weighted velocity of his all-terrain vehicles. Kwan and I were getting pissed. To make things worse, after Darby learned how we had acquired the toy cars, he started telling us about his shitty upbringing and how his Christmas presents were always toys that his mother had saved from cereal boxes and fast-food visits. His mom sounded like a careless bitch and the two of us gave him an earful. In the heat of competition things were said that shouldn't have been said, words no son should tolerate.

We tried finishing the races after he left, but unfortunately serious damage had already been done. Somewhere along the way the dream had soured and our competitive spirits had gotten the better of us. Soon Victor started trash-talking by insisting that we call him Victor-*ious* for the rest of the night. And Kwan, in an act of poor sportsmanship, went about collecting every car for himself. As for me, I retreated to the backroom to gather up and return the tampered boxes to the shelf. Pushing the cart back to the breakfast aisle, I couldn't help but feel a bit guilty. Thanks to Darby, thoughts of ruining some kid's Christmas were circling in my head.

¢¢¢

The next night a loud hammering noise shot up the stairwell. Three succinct blasts while the store was closed, the doors were locked, and I was alone in Tom's office running the daily reports. My heart jumped. Total sales for the day was poor again, worse than Tuesday, barely breaking thirty thousand.

I went downstairs and Tom was standing outside the main entrance. He was out-of-uniform, wearing a gray hooded sweatshirt, jeans, and a pair of white sneakers. Seeing my boss this late at the store was surprising. I unlocked the glass doors to let him in.

"Hallelujah," he said. "You're still here."

He slipped inside and hurried down the side hall to the men's john. I wasn't sure if I should wait for him. But then the door swung open and he was back in the main lobby, buttoning his fly with a pair of clean wet hands.

"Out of paper towels," he said. "Where's Darby?"

"It was a slow night. I sent him home a couple of hours ago. Guess he forgot."

"How slow?"

"Thirty-one-five."

"*Thirty-one-five?*"

I nodded, and Tom went back down the hall to the custodial closet between the two bathrooms. He was making a racket, stirring push-brooms and metal dustpans, eventually returning to the main lobby with nothing but an empty cardboard box.

"We need to order more towels," he said. "Those darn health inspectors will shut us down if customers got no towels to wipe their hands with. Better pull a few rolls off the shelf."

On our way to the paper aisle, he stopped every few feet to primp and fluff displays that had already been primped and fluffed. He played with the corners of potato chip bags. He made sure every spaghetti sauce label was facing out. It was petty, petty stuff. Every few feet he'd be mumbling to himself, about what I had no idea. At one point I thought I heard him say his daughter's name, Traci, but with the next breath I'm pretty sure he said the lobster tank needed cleaning.

When we got to the paper towel section he stood with a bit lip, studying the options like a kid in a candy store. He couldn't make up his mind. Finally I pulled a roll of the generic brand and handed it to him. He took it and a couple more, dropping them in the cardboard box he was still carrying. Then I followed him back to the main lobby.

I stayed by the main doors, unlocking them, while he went into the men's bathroom and set a roll on the sink counter. Then he rapped on the women's bathroom door before entering and setting a roll on their counter too. It was late and I wanted to go home. The clock on the wall read a little past one.

"Aren't you opening in the morning?" I said when he reappeared. "Shouldn't you get some sleep?"

Tom ripped open the third roll of paper towels and began wiping down the side bumper of the shopping cart corral.

"Tom?"

"Huh?"

I slid open the glass doors and nodded to his car parked out front. "I have to finish the reports upstairs. Do you want me to keep the doors unlocked so you can leave?"

Tom pulled himself up off the floor, but kept his eyes on the black bumper running behind and around the two columns of shopping carts. He was thinking.

"Tom?"

"We need more skin colors," he said.

"Huh?"

"We need a better holiday. All we got next month is Father's Day and Flag Day. Those don't cut it. We need a real holiday - something ethnic - like Cinco de Mayo. Any ideas?"

"Nothing in June," I said. "How about November ninth?"

"What's November ninth??"

"The day the Wall was torn down. It's also my birthday."

Tom considered it, looking around, scanning the ceiling, the floors. "Celebrating destruction," he muttered. "Not on my watch. Hand me your keys and I'll leave them in my desk drawer for tomorrow afternoon."

"What about the reports?"

"Don't worry about the reports. I'll finish the reports. Just give me the keys and I'll do the rest."

"You sure?"

He held out his hand while staring at the bumper. "Go on home," he said. "Get some sleep."

I gave him the keys and he went down the hall to the custodial closet. He came back with a squirt bottle. Kneeling down and mumbling to himself, he soaked the black bumper with cleaning solvent.

I stepped outside, slid the doors closed behind me. Then I tapped on the glass until Tom nodded, shuffled across the floor on his knees and turned the latch.

"Don't forget the reports," I shouted through the locked doors. I squatted down to meet him at eye level. "The registers still need to be reset. You need to do it soon."

Tom narrowed his eyes at me – like he didn't understand. Then, with his thumbnail, he scraped a piece of scotch tape off the glass.

SCHADENFREUDE

DEMOLITION STARTED that morning as planned. Posted orange signs up and down Watson said traffic delays should be expected for the rest of the year. The road crew arrived with their excavators, their wood chippers, jackhammers and diesel trucks. Every day they'd start at seven and continue on, in pattern-less drones, until long after I'd head for work.

Wes Steckler, a tenant who lived in the corner unit opposite mine, had been awoken in much the same way. The air, this autumn morning, felt crisp and damp. He was standing outside his door in his bathrobe and wraparound sunglasses, both hands outstretched and clutching the second floor railing. Glaring up at a flat gray sky, over treetops in the noise's general direction, he at last dropped his shoulders and said, "What the fuck?"

He worked nights for an express shipping company, driving a forklift through congested areas at near unimaginable speeds. I know this because one time, in response to his own suggestion, I stopped by to fill out an application. Forklifts were everywhere. It was like watching a mechanical ballet. I didn't know where to stand.

"They're cutting down trees," I said over a beeping truck. "They're putting in bike lanes, widening the road."

"Bike lanes?" Steckler repeated. "Fuck those pedal-pushers. I need my sleep."

He went back inside at the same time I realized what day it was. Down below in the parking lot stood Berndt and Emerick, two kid brothers from a unit on the ground floor, razzing, whipping one another with beach towels. Both were barefoot and shirtless, no doubt killing time until a cab arrived to take them to their weekly swim lesson.

Their usual cabdriver we hated. Steckler once threatened him with a stick. Every Wednesday the insensitive bastard would rip into the parking lot, tires bouncing, front bumper scraping, blasting his horn to get his customers' attention. Never under any circumstance would he go to their door. In the driver's seat he'd be smoking, fumes spilling through the open window of his beat-up sedan, at times a rolled sleeve, a hairy forearm jutting out.

Now it was past ten and the kids were still waiting. The older one, Emerick, stood at the edge of the parking lot while the younger one threw stones at his reflection in a puddle.

I went downstairs to talk to their mother.

The door was wide open and everywhere was a mess. The couch-bed in the living room was pulled out and unmade, with toys, video games and dirty laundry strewn about the carpet. On the kitchen counter sat an oversized TV blaring a colorful game show, next to a sink faucet running a steady stream over a slew of dirty cups and dishes piled high and risking collapse.

I turned down the TV, shut off the water, then stepped over the clutter to the end of the hall. The whole place smelled like vinegar. Knocking softly before cracking open the bedroom door, I got no response except from a brown tabby who slipped through the opening and raced across my foot. The cat didn't belong to them. It was one of the strays who lived behind the complex, under the Dumpster.

The room was small, taken up by a queen-sized mattress, without a frame or a box-spring, and a wooden crib jam-packed with old computers and junky electronic equipment. The closet door was open and spewing clothes and high-heels, while on the bed, curled in a ball under a single white sheet, was the woman I'd secretly been obsessing about for the last three years.

"Mutti," I whispered, but she didn't move. I could see bits of her black hair sprawled across the pillow. One hand hung limp above her head, with fingernails chipped and unpainted, a bulky watch hanging loose on her wrist and flashing zeros.

Remarkably all was quiet inside this room, you could barely detect the revving of a chainsaw behind her screened window. I stood there for a moment, watching her sleep, when out of nowhere both kids stumbled into the apartment, shattering the silence and sending me a jolt. The two moved without regard, thrashing their bodies like a pair of wild salmon caught in the shallows, knocking cereal bowls off the coffee table and spilling milk all over, laughing then pushing and whipping one another until the little one ran to me screaming. Their rowdiness shook through the entire apartment, the ball on the bed started to squirm, her hand dropping behind the pillow. Gently I closed the bedroom door, crept away and herded the noisemakers back outside.

Upstairs I had them wait outside my apartment with instructions not to move. The left half of my face hurt like hell and I wanted to check it in the bathroom mirror. The reflection wasn't what I had expected. Overnight the garish bruise had traveled across my cheek in hues of red, green and purple. Jagged veins trickled across the whites of my eyeball, making it look pink and inflamed. Certain spots I touched, wincing in pain, the whole time focusing, never listening for a sound. When I returned to the living room both kids were sitting on the couch, motionless, but each with a smile stretched across his face. Like two little shoplifters caught empty-handed, they were sitting, grinning, beaming. I looked around. All the furniture was there, nothing had been moved. So I swiped my keys off the counter, bundled up both towels and said, "Let's go."

¢¢¢

I give her things, small things, day-old pastries, loaves of bread, dairy products that would otherwise be thrown out because of their expiration dates. I give her items given to me by soliciting vendors, promotional items such as pens, buttons, can openers and cigarette lighters. Trinkets for her, presents for her kids. I give her any damaged goods that we can't put on our shelves but are perfectly fine to eat. I even buy her things. I buy her things but tell her they were given to me for free. Things like macaroni salads from the deli, fresh produce, a roasted chicken, ground coffee beans…

¢¢¢

It had been one of those days when everything inside felt out of balance and nothing was flowing right. Customers were moving through the aisles at irregular speeds, cleanups and price-checks were being called every five minutes. It was one of those days that makes a night manager sick, not because of what is happening, but because of what *could* happen. Given how behaviors inside a grocery store tend to get worse once the sun goes down, a nervous anticipation was building inside me. My stomach was starting to bubble. My mind was becoming a factory of fear.

Darby called me on the intercom shortly before lunch. I'd been hiding for much of the afternoon, avoiding uncomfortable encounters on the main floor by instead cleaning out the walk-in freezer in the backroom. I had just finished pulling out the frozen inventory so that I could sweep the freezer floor and begin the process of reorganizing. Two pallets of ice cream, one pallet of crushed ice, and countless cases of fruits, vegetables, and dinner trays were sitting at room temperature. Already you could hear things crackling, defrosting. I had to move fast. Time was a consideration.

"We got a live one by the greeting cards," Darby told me when I picked up. "I think he's hammered, a total drunk. You better get over here quick. I can see two bottles peeking out of his jacket."

I hung up the phone and went out to the main floor, made a passing glance up the card aisle. There he was, just like Darby had said, a total drunk swaying, teetering, wrestling to stay upright. Big, bald and unshaven, he had on a leather jacket and was dangling an empty shopping basket.

Darby spotted me from behind the floral counter

and waved me over.

"What should we do?" he said. "Can I confront him? He's got two bottles of beer in his pocket, I watched him do it, so I should probably be the one confronting him, don't you think? What if he's got a warrant? Maybe I'll get to testify."

Darby loved catching shoplifters. He was always keeping an eye out for someone to bust. For him it was the added element of danger, the chance for a courtesy clerk to turn the mundane into the extraordinary. Catch a shoplifter and an otherwise forgettable night instantly becomes legendary. Your confidence swells along with your ego, in your mind you become invincible, and you start craving more. Like an addict you sponge up the rewards and forget about the risks. You forget about the intangibles. Soon you show a willingness to gamble your life for the inconsequential, the trivial, a bottle of beer.

"Slow down," he had me saying. "We have to be careful. We don't know who we're dealing with."

But Darby was too fired up. When our suspect dropped a greeting card back on the shelf and continued on to another aisle, disappearing from view, Darby moved to a new stakeout position at the other end of the store, leaving me to guard the main doors. All this was fine by me. On this particular night I didn't feel like being a leader, an instigator, or even a hero for that matter. A simple night was all I wanted, one with no frills or excitement, one that ran smooth and ended without injury.

I was still behind the floral counter when our suspect appeared at the front of the soup aisle, basket in hand, and made his move for the sliding glass doors. He skirted a couple of displays before staggering across the main lobby, moving fast, never once checking to see if anyone was watching. Both hands he kept at his sides, eyes pointed to the floor.

The automatic doors slid open and I hurried to keep pace with him, fully expecting Darby to round the corner and take control of the situation. But Darby wasn't there, he wasn't anywhere, and now our suspect was getting away. So quickly, in an effort to slow him down, I reached out, grabbing the lip of his shopping basket, and said, "Excuse me, sir," when without warning the man turned and slammed his fist into the side of my head. It was a hard, smashing shot that slowed time while improving the senses. I felt everything; he had tufts of hair on his knuckles. I tumbled backwards to the floor, the fluorescent lights went black, and the next thing I knew, an older woman – a customer – was helping me to my feet. She asked me if I was all right, if there was anything I needed. Unsure of where I was or what had happened or how much time had lapsed, I gently touched the side of my face and gaped through the main doors, in time to see Darby – with the closing speed of a lion – chase down our suspect and flatten him like a gazelle in the middle of the parking lot.

¢¢¢

The police were taking forever. Dispatch on the non-emergency line kept telling me that it was an unusually busy night for the County. They'd tell me to hang tight, they'd thank me for my patience. Each time they'd express care without promising much of anything.

We cuffed our suspect to a chair in the PIC office but he wouldn't stop kicking, so we wrapped his feet together with a roll of duct tape. Like a roped calf he continued to fight and squirm until at last he realized it wasn't worth the effort. Sweat trickling from his brow, one eye pointed at the ceiling, he rested his head against the wall as I tried writing up the loss prevention reports.

"You have any identification?" I asked.

He didn't answer.

"What's your name?"

He refused to say.

I dropped the pen for an icepack. The cold pressure against my face instantly reminded me of the freezer in the backroom. Shit, the freezer! Almost an hour had passed since I pulled the product out of the walk-in. Visions of melted ice cream, defrosted veggies, had me running out of the office. I raced down the bread aisle, through the swinging black doors and into the backroom, where to my surprise, not a single piece of frozen product stood where I had left it. I opened the freezer to find, amid the fading haze, all the product crammed inside. Now the freezer was even more of a mess, but at least someone had voluntarily saved the product from spoiling.

It was the meat butcher, Cheryl. She said she'd noticed me earlier working on the freezer and figured I'd been distracted, so she went ahead and moved everything back inside. She was husky-looking with a flattop hairdo, cow blood spattered across her white apron. Not that any of this should matter. At the moment I wanted nothing more than to wrap my arms around her, squeeze, and never let go.

About an hour later a cop finally showed up. He took one look at my eye and asked me what I wanted to do – press charges or send the guy to detox. Like paper or plastic he didn't care which. The choice was mine to make.

"Whatever's easiest," I said.

I followed them outside and watched the cruiser pull away with our tight-lipped suspect in back. The night was cool and quiet, in front of me open asphalt and empty spaces. I stood staring. Of the few parked cars, I noticed one sitting oddly alone in the middle, a beat-up sedan with scratches along the front bumper. Slowly as I moved across the lot, at a pace worthy of my suspicions, the left side of my face started to tingle. Through the front windshield you could see the meter on the dash.

¢¢¢

When I got home that night Steckler was sitting in a collapsible chair outside his apartment, working his way through his second six-pack; he spotted me through the second-floor railing on the other side of the complex.

"What'd you bring her this time, grocery man? Dented soda cans? Bruised honeycrisps?"

The lights were on, it was two in the morning, but nobody was home. I turned from her door and looked up in the direction of Steckler's voice where, to my amazement, his silhouette moved succinctly, deliberately – like a forklift. I watched him drop down, pick up another beer bottle, twist, tilt, then pull.

"Is that you, Steck?"

He set his beer down, shifted in his seat. The grocery bag behind my back grew heavy in my hand.

"Nobody's home," he said. "She's at work, kids are with her. You want me to tell them you stopped by?"

I set down the paper bag and headed for the stairs, pretending not to have heard his question. My legs were tired from walking aisles all day. The sky had broken open, stars were out, but the handrail was still wet from an earlier rain. Each slippery step was freckled with green moss.

The first time we met was at the store, three years ago, when she came in with a WIC check and didn't understand how it worked. She wanted brown eggs instead of white, Swiss cheese instead of cheddar, and was upset that I wouldn't allow these small changes to be made. I tried explaining to her that I had nothing to do with it, that the rules were those of the federal grant program, and strictly enforced so that the store wouldn't get reimbursed if the items didn't match up. But this didn't matter to her. She felt slighted. Clutching both kids in her arms, she ditched the cart in the middle of the aisle and hurried out.

Now Steckler twisted in his chair, beer in hand, watching me cross the opposite landing.

"Why you care about her so much, grocery man? You lonely? You wanna get in her pants?"

I stopped at my front door, focused on finding the right key. His voice carried easily from his side to mine, now that Watson ran quiet without the road crew working away.

"What are you after, Cather? Can't fool a fooler! I know that skank's got you hungry for something!"

It was Steckler's day off; he had nothing better to do than to surf porn and speculate. But his bitter tone combined with how little he knew about me suggested he wasn't as much admonishing my life as he was defending his own. I had no idea what had gotten him so riled up so fast. All I wanted was what he already had: a few beers, a chair, and no one to listen to.

I unlatched the deadbolt, went inside. Before I could close the door, Steckler raised his voice, called out my name. The moment I turned, he made a loud smooching sound with his lips.

¢¢¢

Traffic was at a dead stop. Engines were off. Frustrated drivers leaned on their horns. Some were directing their scowls at me, as if I was the reason for their holdup. What did they expect me to do? The kid was having a tantrum. Lying flat on his back in the middle of the apartment parking lot, Berndt wouldn't stop kicking, squirming, screaming. I tried picking him up but he was impossible to move. It was like his body had been glued to the asphalt. It wasn't my fault we couldn't get to his swim class in time. Blame the guys in the orange vests, I told him. I'm not the one widening the road, adding the goddamn bike lanes.

It was November ninth, my birthday.

Your thirtieth is supposed to shock you into making life-changing decisions. No more fooling around, that voice inside your head now suggests you might want to get serious. Try caring for a change. Risk everything, not for yourself – but for somebody else. Give without the get and trust others will do the same.

    I looked down at Berndt who was still on the ground, crying, screaming, and I wondered how far I could kick him. Meanwhile his older brother, Emerick, kept tugging on my arm, trying to get my attention, saying over and over how everything would be okay if we just swam here in the parking lot. If we just swam here in the parking lot, he bet his brother would probably stop crying. He made it sound so simple, like reality was something we could easily overlook.

    Enough was enough. I grabbed Berndt under both arms and held him out in front of me. He wiggled in my hands, screaming even louder. I had no choice but to put him down.

    Emerick crossed the lot and whistled for our attention. Having mapped the pool's dimensions from corner to corner, he could now point out the boundaries to us. The shallow end, he said, would run from the complex to the first divider. Everywhere else, he insisted, would be a thousand feet deep.

    Another horn honked over a wood chipper grinding its metal teeth as Berndt sat up and surveyed the surroundings, heavy tears still dripping down his face. Deep five-year-old thoughts had him wiping his runny nose with the back of his hand.

"What about the cars?" he whimpered, pointing to each of the four parked inside the waterlines.

"The cars are islands," his older brother said.

Berndt leaned forward, considering this. "What about sharks?"

"Don't worry about sharks," Emerick said. "They're only in the deep end."

"No!" I blurted out. "There are no sharks. The water is too warm for sharks."

"Not for hammerheads," Emerick said. He dipped his foot into a handicapped spot, testing the water. "Hammerheads prefer a warmer climate. They can be found up and down the continental shelf."

The continental shelf? I didn't argue with him – it sounded like he knew what he was talking about. Instead I knelt down next to Berndt and pointed across the water to where the nets would normally be and said that's why the nets were there – to keep the hammerheads away. I asked Berndt if he could see them and he squinted to where I was pointing. "Do you see them, Berndt?" Dear God, I prayed for him to see them. He asked me what the nets were made of and I said, "What do you think?" He said kryptonite and I said, "You'd better believe it."

I took his hand and we waded into the shallow end. The soft current moved with the wind, white light bouncing off the flat gray sky. We let our arms rise with the warm water, above our chests, to our necks. And when three loud blasts rang out from the roadwork down the street, Emerick swam for the nearest island and shouted, "Pirates are coming! Pirates are coming!"

MOSQUITO DRILL

IN THE WEEKS LEADING UP to Leven's disappearance, signs of a mental breakdown were popping up everywhere. His latest fall off the wagon, this time triggered by the smell of barbecue chicken in the air, had the old guy losing control over his limited means. And since he couldn't afford to refill his Librium bottle, his behavior, though always erratic, seemed all the more impulsive and irrational.

It was after two in the morning when I got home from work and found my roommate on the kitchen floor, sifting through the lower cabinets. Shit! Damn! Fuck! – a mounting crisis shot through the entire apartment. Pots and pans were clanging, mixing bowls clamoring, his head and arms buried deep beneath the counter.

"What are you looking for?" I said.

"Cookie tray," he grunted.

"We don't have a cookie tray."

"Then any tray, goddammit!"

I opened the cabinet to his right and pulled out a pizza pan.

"That's perfect," he said, snatching the metal saucer from me. Then he pulled himself up off the floor, face flushed and sweating.

I didn't bother ask what he was making. From the fridge I grabbed a beer and went to the couch in the living room. An infomercial was on television and a mess of tools and empty fast-food containers littered the coffee table. I pulled down my tie, lost the apron, and ridded my keys and box-knife so I could sit however I wanted without getting speared.

In front of me a woman wearing shorts and a tank-top was bouncing on her toes, testing a pair of gelled shoes along a sunny boardwalk. She appeared happy, pleasantly surprised and nodding her head as the camera zoomed in on her smiling face. The man at her side anxiously awaited her verdict. "How do they feel?" he kept asking her. "How do they feel?"

Leven emerged from the kitchen as she was giving her answer. "They're so soft! They feel like pillows!" In his hands were two ice-filled glasses and a half-empty handle of what looked like vodka.

"Where'd you get that?" I said.

"Earnings from our little roundup, remember?" The poor lush gave a smirk. "Your boss almost shit his shorts. Twenty-four grocery carts we rescued from Whitaker's backyard."

I untied my shoes. "Twenty-four, eh?"

He poured generously into both glasses and then sat down in the recliner next to the couch.

"So tell me," he said, "what's your schedule look like this weekend?" He levered up the squeaky ottoman. "You working? Got any plans?"

"I'm off the next two days."

Leven wiped booze from his lips, then licked the side of his finger. "Next week's the Fourth of July and I'm thinking of driving up to Washington for a firework run. You want in? Resell them down here and we'd split the profits. I know some folks in Toppenish who'll put us up for free, no questions asked."

I shook my head, checked the bottom of my foot. Lately I'd been getting these bumps on my feet. I showed them to Leven. "Have you ever seen bumps like this before? They hurt like thumbtacks. Maybe I need new shoes."

"Now hold on," Leven barked. "You even been to Yakama Nation? Goddamn cutest spot around. Full of good culture, good food – you'd be surprised at how much you like it."

I shrugged. "Never been."

"Of course they got a casino there now. You never know what kind of draw that brings." Leven slipped one hand under his shirt to scratch his armpit, careful not to spill his drink. "Used to be a wholesome town, Toppenish. My boy, Rooster, he'd always be catching turtles and selling them in our driveway as pets. No permits, no hassles – it was the perfect place to raise a family."

"I didn't know you had a son."

Leven chewed on some ice, stared at the infomercial. Something he saw on the television had him snapping his fingers. "Shoot, I almost forgot. Your sampler lady stopped by about an hour ago."

"Sampler lady?"

"That one in the deli who needed the braces." He nodded to the latest test-subject bouncing across the screen. Somehow the sight of her jogging in place had reminded him of a girl I used to date. "I forget her name. The one whose teeth were such a goddamned mess before."

"Melinda," I said.

"No, the other one."

"What do you mean? It had to be her."

"How do you know?"

"Because I bought Melinda braces."

"Well, then maybe this girl wasn't the one you bought braces for. Guess I just assumed she was."

"Fine, whatever. What'd she want?"

Leven finished his drink, tried talking with an ice cube in his mouth. "She wanted to show you her teeth."

It was hopeless; the old man really had lost his marbles. A timer beeped in the kitchen and pulled him from his chair; he took his glass and the bottle with him, across the room to the microwave on the counter, where he pulled out a steaming bag of popcorn, thoughtfully pinched between his fingers.

I dropped my foot in exchange for the glass on the table. I gave the booze a sniff. "What is this stuff anyway? It has no smell."

Leven opened the bag of popcorn and spread some across the pizza pan. "They're called blisters." He hiccupped. "You get them from walking on your feet."

¢¢¢

That night we killed a half-case of beer and wound up hunting waterfowl in Dorothy Whitaker's backyard. Instead of using shotguns, Leven insisted we get the ducks drunk off of popcorn and grain alcohol. That's what the pizza pan was for. The idea was to get the pintails so drunk that they'd pass out long enough for us to sneak back later and pluck them off the ground like Easter eggs. Leven said he used to hunt like this outside of Toppenish when they were living there, a long time ago, before the family broke apart and the casino moved in. Back when spotted turtles still swam around the lake.

¢¢¢

Saturday was laundry day. I got back from the Laundromat around three and Darby was sitting outside my front door, reading a sportsmen's catalogue and sipping a Snapple. The nineteen-year-old courtesy clerk glanced up from a section on compound bows and sprang to his feet. He offered to hold my basket of clean clothes while I searched for the key.

"Dang," he said. "You're a good folder."

I unlocked the door, went inside. The apartment still stunk like burnt popcorn. Empty beer cans and leftover kernels lay scattered across the living room floor.

"What are you doing here?" I said.

Darby set the laundry basket on the recliner and pulled a VHS cassette from under his belt. "I brought the movie I was telling you about. You know, *The Deserter*. Ricardo Montalban plays the role of Natachai, an Indian friend who's also a scout for the army. It's a flawless performance, one you have to see. This copy's a little warped, so you can keep it as long as you want."

"Isn't Montalban Mexican?"

"Yeah," Darby said. "The man's a chameleon."

On the kitchen counter the voicemail light was blinking, so I went over and pressed the button. The message was from Leven and had been taken two hours earlier:

"Hey there, Dale. Beautiful day out here in Toppenish, yes sir, a real snapshot... Long story short I could use a little help. Was wondering if you could pick me up, I know, I know, it's short notice and you got things you need to do... But if you could pick me up tomorrow, that'd be great, real great, you don't have to call or nothing. Just take the eighty-four to the ninety-seven and meet me by the mural in the middle. I'll keep an eye out for ya. Thanks a bunch, pal. Means a lot."

The message ended and the blinking light shut off. I opened my eyes. On the counter, next to the phone, was Leven's empty Librium bottle.

"I know Toppenish," Darby said. "Me and my step-dad used to go arrowhead hunting there on the weekends. Back then you could make a lot of money arrowhead hunting. We didn't find any up there, but in Moab my step-dad got arrested. Turns out arrowhead hunting's illegal – it's a federal offense. Sure, they dropped the arrowhead charge and got him on dope, but can you believe that bullshit?"

I pushed back from the counter, went around to the fridge. "How am I supposed to pick Leven up? He has the goddamn truck. I swear the guy's got dementia. He's completely flipped his lid."

"What's dementia?"

I pulled out a carton of orange juice and took a heavy swig. A cold burst of citrus went straight to my stomach. "Remember that one customer who took a shit on the backroom floor because he couldn't find the bathroom?" I belched. "That was dementia."

"You mean the guy with the kilt? I wasn't there. It was that other kid… What was his name? He said you paid him twenty bucks to clean up the mess. I forget his name. What was his name again?"

The room fell silent, nothing could be heard but the ticking clock on the living room wall. I stood inside the fridge's open door, drinking orange juice amid the spiral of cool air, when without warning an unpleasant sound, coming from down the hall, squeezed my stomach like a vice:

"Barrhh-aap!"

Orange juice crawled up the back of my throat.

"What was that?" Darby said.

"Barrhh-aap!"

The noise was coming from behind the bathroom door. Curious, Darby disappeared down the hall, then returned a few seconds later with a sick-looking duck cradled in his arms.

"Look what I found in your tub," he said. "He scared the living shit out of me. I thought he was a football."

"It's a girl," I corrected.

"A girl? How do you know?"

"She has brown feathers."

Darby looked concerned, combing the duck's feathers with his fingertips. He tried making eye contact with her, but for a duck with a serious hangover, she didn't seem interested.

"How long have you had her?"

"She's not mine. She's not anybody's."

The open bag of popcorn was still resting on the counter. Darby grabbed a handful to see if she wanted any. She didn't.

"When was the last time you fed her? She looks pretty sick."

"I haven't fed her anything."

"Not even a cracker?"

"She's wild, Darby."

The duck closed her eyes, buried her beak under a wing. Who could blame her? The thought of eating popcorn was enough to make *me* sick.

"Maybe I should take her," Darby said. "Give her some food, nurse her back to health. I'll put her on the front porch so she can fly away whenever she's feeling better..."

"Do whatever you want."

"You don't care?"

"Knock yourself out."

Darby headed for the open door with the duck asleep in his arms, but stopped before stepping outside.

"You know," he said, "I have a car. Tomorrow I could go out there and pick Leven up. It doesn't bother me. I got nothing better to do."

"No way."

"Why not?"

"Because it's not your problem. Leven needs to figure this one out on his own." I handed Darby his hunting catalogue and urged him out the door.

¢¢¢

Early the next morning I called Darby and told him to meet me in the store parking lot. When I spotted him, a sharp glare from the rising sun bounced off the roof of his most prized possession, a 1976 steel blue Chrysler Cordoba. A sizeable dent stood out along the left rear fender, but otherwise the classic coupe's lines were clean. Its original owner was a regular customer who before dying had sold Darby the car for next to nothing. The miles were low and the numbers all matched, but what really mattered to Darby was that the Corinthian leather, a feature infamously noted in a seventies car commercial by none other than the great Ricardo Montalban, had maintained its rich cushiony feel.

"Christian Lemke!" Darby shouted across the lot. "The kid who cleaned up that guy's shit in the backroom... Christian *fucking* Lemke!"

"That's right," I said. "He played badminton."

"No, I think it was squash."

"Same thing. What's in there?" I nodded to the cardboard box sitting on the trunk with a giant green leaf sticking out the top.

"You mean, Georgiana?" He pulled the box down to show me. Nestled inside, among a random collection of leaves and twigs, was the duck. A white plastic bag lined the very bottom, with a small bowl of water twist-tied and taped to one corner.

"I left her out on the porch last night, thinking she'd fly away at some point. I don't know what's wrong with her. She's eating again, stopped making that weird burping noise. Maybe she just likes me."

Or, I thought, she could have brain damage.

Darby opened the passenger-side door and flipped forward the front seat. Gently he tried squeezing the cardboard box in back. But there was a problem: it was too big and wouldn't fit.

"Stop it," I said. "I'll sit in back."

"You sure?"

I grabbed the headrest and ducked inside. The buttoned upholstery, soft and warm to the touch, breathed like a cheap polyester sleeping bag.

¢¢¢

The drive out to Toppenish takes about three hours. Cruising east along the eighty-four with the windows down, a clear blue sky above us, the powerful Columbia River gliding smoothly with very little wind, we couldn't have asked for better conditions on this random excursion of ours. It felt good to get away. But then, twenty minutes into the drive, Darby started talking and wouldn't shut up. Natural landmarks and scatter-brained thoughts had him blabbing the entire time. There was so much to see, so much to take in, so much going on around us that he'd hardly give himself time to breathe. He'd point out every telephone pole with an osprey nest. He'd peer up at the tall basalt cliffs that lined the river's southern banks and speculate on how long it took for them to get that way. Somewhere in the middle he started confessing his own dreams, he'd romanticize his life... He would try imagining the day when he and his pretend wife would take their pretend kids to the top of every waterfall – but first he needed a girlfriend – so maybe he'd learn how to windsurf so he could meet her out on the water, one blustery day... They were simple fantasies, harmless flights of whimsy, none that were hard to listen to if only he had skipped the part where he'd turn to me and say, "You know what I mean?" Like he needed my validation after every delusion. "What an awesome job to drive a train, you get to see the country, travel the world... you know what I mean?" "Kite surfing doesn't scare me. Paragliding doesn't either. I don't want to be afraid of anything. Fear to me is God's way of saying, 'Give it a try'... you know what I mean?" "If I were a bird I'd live out here. That way you wouldn't have to flap around so much. Just jump off a cliff, open your wings and let the wind push you to where you wanna go... you know what I mean?"

In the backseat pocket I found a copy of Ricardo

Montalban's *Reflections: A Life in Two Worlds.* In his memoir the Hollywood star writes, "that only through discipline can you achieve freedom. Pour water in a cup and you can drink from it. Without a cup the water would splash all over. The cup is discipline."

Someone had highlighted this excerpt.

¢¢¢

Finding Leven we soon realized wouldn't be that easy. Toppenish, a place I had never been to let alone heard of, proved much bigger than I had anticipated. Self-lauded on area billboards as The City of Murals and Museums, home to seventy wall paintings and, for what it's worth, the nation's only Agricultural Hop Museum, the town stood alone but proud in the sprawling wine hills of the Yakima Valley. By no means a metropolis, Toppenish did have enough pull to boast an annual rodeo and a nearby Indian casino.

"Welcome to Paradise," Darby said as we pulled up to one of the few stoplights. Through the windshield he admired the painted murals and authentic-looking western storefronts lining both sides of the street. "Looks the same from what I remember. Where's the old man supposed to meet us at?"

"He said somewhere in the middle."

The light turned green and Darby continued down Toppenish Avenue and across the railroad tracks. He turned left on Division Street, cut back onto West 1st Street, drove a few blocks down to South Elm, took another right, to Washington Avenue, then swung back around to the front of City Hall. The entire circle covered most of the city's center, but none of the outskirts or residential streets.

"He could be anywhere," I said after the first lap. "It's getting hot back here. Pull over and let me out."

For the next thirty minutes we walked through town, checking every tavern and restaurant without any luck. Back in the car we broadened the circle, so as not to overlook the town's hospital, the community swimming pool, the Mount Adams public golf course and, of course, the casino. But there was no sign of him in any of these places. Our search, however thorough, had yielded nothing. There was not a wisp of Leven or the truck anywhere in Toppenish.

We stopped to eat lunch in the shadow of the town's water tower. With no breeze the afternoon sun hammered down and slow-cooked the Cordoba into a crock-pot. I wouldn't dare get back inside. Closing my eyes, lying back on the grass, I felt no urge, no responsibility to anyone but myself. Darby stood up and suggested we make a change. He noticed a banner in front of the Toppenish Chamber of Commerce that advertised a horse-drawn mural tour. He had the guts to call it our lucky break.

"Don't be ridiculous," I said.

"C'mon, we'll hit all the sites."

"No way. No wagon rides."

"Why not? You scared?"

"No, Darby, I'm not scared."

"Then what's your problem?"

"I don't have a problem."

"So why not?"

"Because."

"Because why?"

"Because I don't feel like it, okay?"

"Fine then. Guess I'll go alone."

"Don't forget the duck."

"It could be a while."

"Is that a promise?"

"You'll be sorry."

"I already am."

¢¢¢

In his memoir, Ricardo Montalban regards the mind as a computer, "the most intricate and sensitive computer ever constructed. Nothing that is fed into that computer is ever totally forgotten. We think that we are creating new ideas, but in reality we are only compiling information that we have already absorbed. If that information is warped and self-centered, then your mind will follow the same configuration. But if your upbringing has known freedom tempered with discipline, your computer will provide a similar result."

I got back in the crock-pot at a quarter past two and drove through the center of Toppenish. Again nothing turned up so I stretched the circle a little more, this time weaving through the quaint residential streets and suburbs. The further out I went the more desolate my surroundings became; soon barren fields and arid farmland soaked every angle.

Alongside an unpaved road I noticed a cardboard sign nailed to an oak tree. It had a crooked arrow and the word "KA-BOOM!" spray-painted in red.

I went ahead and turned down the grooved road, letting a plume of dust kick up behind me, gravel crunching under the Cordoba's spoked wheels. A sorry-looking vegetable patch stretched along the left side of the road, while to my right a gully of dry grass led to a tall line of maples and cottonwoods. Beyond their swaying branches ran shimmering glimpses of the Yakima River.

Up about fifty yards shuddered another piece of flimsy cardboard, this one with an arrow pointing into the gully. I stopped before the sign, looked down at the narrow stretch of lowland between the road and the trees, to a makeshift stand built out of plywood and crudely painted in red, white and blue. Parked next to it was an old camper hitched to a pickup truck with an ATV in back. No one was around. The entire operation appeared empty, abandoned.

    I drove the Cordoba down the slope to a circle of shaved grass, and parked. The wind was heavy; grass seed and pollen dust floated through the air. I opened the door and got out of the car. There was no noise other than a few birds and the river's whitewater rushing beyond the tree-line.

    I walked up to the counter to see if anyone was around. An array of fireworks were stacked and hung along the back wall. Among those being displayed were roman candles, m-80s, m-1000s, cherry bombs, smoke bombs, bottle rockets, sky rockets, ground spinners and fountains, black snakes and pinwheels, sparklers, some with names in Spanish and Japanese. An open box of fried chicken rested on a plastic crate, next to a radio turned low and two fold-up chairs sitting empty in the corner.

    POP!

    A distant shot echoed through the sky. I turned my head in the direction of the sound and a string of three more – POP, POP, POP! - shot out from behind the wooden stand.

    A group of angry voices, howling with disappointment, also carried in the wind, before being swallowed by a sharp valley gust ruffling the little flags taped to the stand's awning.

Around the corner, at a distance the length of a football field, I spotted four guys hovering shirtless around a picnic table. They were laughing, joking, with their backs turned to me; one guy was sitting at the table with a rifle up against his shoulder.

Looking upwind through a pair of binoculars, one of the spectators made a signal with his arm. The laughing stopped, more awkward silence followed… POP! Another bullet ripped across the river valley.

The man sitting at the table slammed his fist in frustration, swung out his legs and exchanged the rifle he was holding for a can of beer. Another guy took his place. He sat down, they all hovered. Then came more of that silence, nothing but the sound of whitewater, a few birds, and then – POP! – another gunshot.

One try was all he needed. The rifleman dropped the gun, pumping his fist high in the air. The group roared their approval, passing high-fives around the table. What they were shooting at, I couldn't tell from where I was standing, but three of them headed toward the undisclosed target, while the remaining one broke away and strutted toward me. With his shaved head pointed at the ground as he walked, it took him a while to notice me waiting by the stand.

And even then he showed little regard. Smoking a cigarette, he had a thin mustache and tattoos covering his chiseled arms and upper body. His jeans were faded and hanging loosely around a white pair of briefs. He had a red bandanna tucked in his front pocket.

I waited at the counter, expecting him to acknowledge me when he stepped inside. But he didn't. Instead, with the burning cigarette pinched in the corner of his mouth, he went straight to the plastic crate in the corner. He pulled out a twenty-pound sack of potatoes and flung it over his shoulder. Then he walked out – like I didn't exist.

He went to the pickup truck and got something out of the glove compartment. When he slammed the door and started to walk away, a strange knocking noise came from inside the attached camper. At first I figured it was a dog or some kind of animal trying to get out – until the sack of potatoes dropped to the ground and the man shot one glance at the rundown camper, then another at me.

My heart jumped. The knocking had stopped, but the guy was giving me a stone-cold glare. I noticed a padlock on the front door of the camper. Why was there a padlock? Was it locked or unlocked? I couldn't tell. Is that normal? To have a padlock on a camper door?

"Play on down!" the man shouted.

I didn't understand. "Sorry?"

The man took a step forward. "Play on down!"

Again he tossed the bag of potatoes over his shoulder and turned to walk away. The tattoo on his back had an angel with wings. He got about halfway to the picnic table when the knocking resumed, though this time much louder, so loud in fact that it sounded desperate and more like pounding. The camper's wooden side panels started to tremble and the man, seeing this, dropped the potatoes and raced back toward the camper. He slapped the sidewall hard with an open hand and the knocking instantly stopped. Then he backed away, toward me, and now I could see the tattoo plain as day. Across his back, shoulder to shoulder and down the spine, was an angel wielding a bloody sword, and the word APOCALYPSE scrawled along his waist.

There was no way for me to turn and run. Both knees had locked, my legs felt posted to the ground. He turned to face me as the others waited and watched by the picnic table. What was he doing? Did he forget something? Maybe he was getting another weapon – a knife, some rope – such were the objects running through my head. The knocking sound had stopped, but now my heart was beating louder than ever.

I stood with bunched fists.

"You need something?" he said.

"Huh?"

"Know what the fuck you want?" He looked over my shoulder at the parked Cordoba. "Oregon, huh? We got more shit packed away, better stuff you might wanna look at."

I glanced over at his friends who were watching from the picnic table. One of them was studying us with a pair of binoculars; another one had the rifle clutched in both hands.

"You gonna buy shit or what?" the man asked.

Leven said Toppenish was a beautiful place. A good place to work, a great place to raise a family. I could hear his voice now. I wanted so bad to believe him. I had imagined his memories, put faith in them, and now they were dying.

The man took one last drag from his cigarette before flicking it in the dirt. Then he pulled the red bandanna from his pocket and wiped sweat off the top of his head.

"Fucking heat," he said. "I hate this shit."

"You mean – you're not from Toppenish?"

The man, tilting back his head, didn't respond at first. He just stood there, quietly. Like he had options.

¢¢¢

Back under the town's water tower, another hour had passed before Darby emerged in high spirits. He knew nothing about the whereabouts of Leven or the truck, but the tour he said was fantastic. The wagon ride covered the town's entire collection of wall murals and gave fascinating insight to their making as well as to the region's history.

"Every June," he said, "they add a new mural. We just missed it by a few days. It's a huge event. They say people come from all over to watch the paint dry."

It was late afternoon, the hottest point in the day. We circled the city's center one last time, checking again every restaurant and tavern before ultimately stopping at the police station. We knew we couldn't file a missing person's report this early, nor could we say for sure that Leven really was missing, but we did leave our names and contact information in the event that someone meeting his description happened to turn up. We figured it was the least we could do.

Darby opened the door and we went back out into the sun. He had left the cardboard box with the duck in a shady spot along the sidewalk. I had told him the damn thing would fly away, but Darby, nonetheless, seemed surprised to find the box empty. Dumping the leaves, twigs and grass into a nearby trash can, he didn't say a word at first; you could tell his mind was processing. He scanned the street in both directions, squinted up at the empty sky. Then he tossed me the keys and said, "You drive. I want to keep the box."

¢¢¢

The drive home was quiet. We were on the eighty-four, following the Columbia back to Portland, when I thought of a story Christian Lemke told me after cleaning shit off the backroom floor.

One summer, when he was nine, he had gone to a camp somewhere in the Midwest. He spent four weeks there, which would've been fine had it not been for a couple of counselors working there. In Lemke's cabin was this hyperactive kid who was always breaking the rules and causing problems. He was constantly fucking up. Finally two of the counselors got fed up and dragged him out of the cabin in the middle of the night. They made the kid strip down to his underwear and stand alone in the middle of the baseball field. It was summertime, humid, and the bugs were always swarming at night. Three minutes was always the starting point. The kid had to stand still for three minutes without moving, as each counselor aimed his flashlight at him to attract the mosquitoes. If during that time he moved a muscle, even twitched a finger, the counselors would tack on another minute. It was pure torture; Lemke and the other campers would watch from their windows. Sometimes the kid would be out there for hours, slapping away, mosquitoes landing on his eyes, his lips, but by far the worst, supposedly, were his feet. When you're standing in one spot for that long all the blood goes to your legs, so that's where the mosquitoes want to go. They'll land on a vein and just sit there, sit there until they almost explode.

Lemke said the kid was the toughest motherfucker he'd ever met. He wore those bites on his body like badges of honor. Rather than shape up and learn from his mistakes, the kid only got worse and by the fourth week, he was making bets with other campers on how long he could last. One day, during rest period, Lemke caught the kid poking his feet with a needle. When Lemke asked him what he was doing, the kid said he was getting himself ready, making himself numb.

Now the sky was getting dark and we still had an hour left in the drive. Darby had his eyes closed, legs stretched across the backseat. I thought he was asleep, but then he spoke up.

"I heard Leven got arrested once for shooting a sea lion. Is that true? Why would you ever shoot a sea lion?"

I looked in the rearview mirror at him staring out at the Columbia, at the black rolling hills lining the north bank. "Same reason you might pull a weed or attack a virus, I guess. Whatever gets in your way."

The dim stretch of water surged alongside us, until a wall of concrete cut against the current, whitewater roaring beneath the floodgates of the Bonneville Dam. Water tumbled through the chutes and into the afterbay, swirling, rolling out steady then pushing forward downriver at a managed pace, flat and even, smooth like the road.

BEAT SUNSET

She walked into the PIC office, shaken. It was the day before the big game. Tom was yelling on the phone as Carlos sat at his desk, eating a teriyaki bowl for a midmorning snack. The freight load hadn't arrived yet and it was over eight hundred pieces. The old store director wanted to know where the truck was and the explanation he was getting didn't seem up to snuff. He shook his head, squeezed the back of his neck. He slammed down the phone and turned to his grocery manager, red in the face.

"Heads are gonna roll, you hear me? We can't tolerate this kind of sloppiness. It's ridiculous. Our livelihood's at the mercy of an idiot truck driver!"

Carlos shrugged, wiped his mouth with a napkin. Then he turned to Shelly in the doorway, which made Tom turn too.

"Hey there, Shortstop," Tom said with a much softer tone. "What are you doing here? Your shift doesn't start for another hour."

Shelly grabbed the lip of the door, gently closing it behind her. Her broad shoulders tightened as her unassuming brown eyes danced about the room.

"Where's Darby?" she said. "We need to get Darby, right away. This isn't good. This isn't good at all."

"Shit." By accident Carlos had spilled some marinated rice in his lap. "He's upstairs on his break. Why? What did he do this time?"

"No, no, it's nothing like that." Shelly wrung her hands like they were cold or wet. "I was just outside and saw that chemistry teacher, Mister Mattworth, drive up. He's over in the bakery with a shopping cart."

"Mattworth's here?" Carlos stood up and went to the window in the door. He peered through the glass but, seeing nothing, turned back to Shelly and said, "Are you sure?"

"One hundred percent. Same car and everything."

"Who's Mattworth?" Tom said.

Carlos opened the door and touched Shelly's arm. He could barely wrap his hand around her sculpted bicep.

"Go upstairs," he told her. "Go upstairs and distract him. Don't let him anywhere near the main floor. I'll call you on the intercom when Mattworth's gone. And move fast. Darby has only a few minutes left on his break."

Shelly stepped away and across the row of check-stands, in the direction of the stairwell leading up to the break room. Outside the doorway Carlos stood on his toes, staring out at the bakery, when Tom called him back into the office.

"What the heck's going on?"

Carlos pushed the door to a crack. "You remember Mattworth. He's the guy who supposedly, you know, the guy who became friends with Darby and, you know…"

Tom's eyes widened. "He's *here*? I thought he was a war-game coordinator or something – not a chemistry teacher."

"He's both, or he was. Mattworth's the reason Darby went to high school out of district. Since the kid wouldn't talk, they couldn't fire the bastard. It's why Darby took a city bus across the river for three years."

Tom went to the window. "You mean this pervert's been teaching in my daughter's school? How come I didn't know this?"

"He's semi-retired, teaches part-time now. Honors chemistry, I think."

"And we're sure it's him?"

"He's been in here before. Dale kicked him out a while back. Trespassed him, I think, but that only lasts a year."

"Baloney," Tom said. "He's testing us. This guy knows he can't be anywhere near this property."

The old store director went to the coat-rack and

started digging through his jacket. He pulled out his car keys and told Carlos to get Erin, the store's head checker, on the intercom.

Carlos picked up the intercom, pressed the black button. "Erin intercom, please!" His amplified voice shot across the entire store.

"Give her the reins," Tom said. "Tell her she's in control. Make sure every department head is where they should be. Call all courtesy clerks up front. Nobody argues, nobody complains. Get those lines covered and then meet me out back."

¢¢¢

Shelly Briggs had the strongest arm on the field. It's what drew the scouts, won close games. She and Tom's daughter, Traci, were called the Dynamic Duo in the local paper. By the end of her freshman season big colleges were already offering her four-year scholarships. But by her senior year those offers were long gone. She still had the arm, but somewhere along the way, she had lost control. It was as inexcusable as it was inexplicable. Scouts wouldn't go near her. Too erratic, they'd say.

Too wild.

She decided to take a year off after graduation and get back to basics. Her family hired a trainer and Tom gave her a checking job at the store. Over the upcoming summer she hoped to raise the eyebrows of some of those scouts who had passed on her. This was her plan. Everybody knew this.

Now, when she walked into the break room, Darby surprised Shelly by lobbing an apple for her to catch. He was sitting on the couch with the TV turned so he could lean back and stretch out his legs. She snagged the airborne Granny Smith with one hand and he said, "Now throw it back." Behind him was a window overlooking the store's main floor.

Gently she tossed back the apple, underhanded. Darby reached out to catch it but it slipped through his fingers and dropped on the dirty tile floor. He picked it up, rubbed his dessert clean with the hem of his apron, then took a giant bite.

"What'chya watching?" Shelly pulled a chair from the lunch-table, straddled it backwards with her arms folded across the seatback. "*Bonanza?*"

"*Little House*," Darby said with a mouthful of apple. "I always catch the second half during my lunch break." Then he looked up at the clock, puzzled. "What are you doing here already?"

"My little brother has a doctor's appointment so my mom had to drop me off early. Nothing serious, just a checkup. His seizures have been getting better with the new medication."

"That's good news." Darby took two more chunks out of the apple before tossing the core at the garbage can next to the sink. He missed. Shelly reached down and pinched the stem, flinging it in the basket for him.

The episode was to be continued. When the end credits rolled across the television, Darby got up off the couch and stretched. Shelly loosened her grip on the chair and said, "Where are you going? Don't leave yet. I need to ask a favor, you know, get your opinion on something."

In truth Shelly had no idea what she needed. But being a good shortstop is also about thinking fast on your feet. She stood up, crossed the room, to the bulletin board pinned with random flyers.

"Have you ever called this number before?"

It was a public service announcement for a suicide hotline. The picture had a depressed-looking guy standing on a bridge walkway. *Need someone to talk to? Call us. We care.*

"Me?" Darby smirked. "Why would I kill myself?"

It was a good question. Why would anyone kill themselves? Only the weak-minded would ever consider calling it quits. Which was exactly Shelly's problem. Throwing a ball from third to first used to be second-nature. Maybe the mental block wasn't a glitch. Maybe her mind really was broken.

"I wonder," she said, "if Tom put this up for someone in particular. Can you think of anyone around here who might be suicidal? Kwan? Maybe Victor?"

Darby thought about it. "Maybe Victor. He's

got a real short fuse. But I always figured he'd bomb this place with him inside. More of a murder-suicide, which still qualifies, I guess."

Shelly touched the poster, closed her eyes. She tried imagining a scout sitting alone in the bleachers. Her trainer swings the bat, sends an easy one in her direction. The grounder bounces into her mitt, she takes one step, grips the ball, whips the sucker high over the first baseman's head.

Darby turned to the clock on the wall. "I better get going." Down the hallway he went, almost to the stairs, when Shelly blinked and called out his name.

He stopped in the doorway. "What is it?"

She turned to him, glossy-eyed.

The air inside the break room was stagnant. The dirty lunch-table had stains and crumbs everywhere. The couch was so old and disgusting that Darby was the only person who'd use it, and the refrigerator, full of forgotten lunches, smelled rotten and needed cleaning out. She hated everything about this room. To her it felt like a dungeon. That's why she always took her breaks outside the store. Didn't matter how cold it was, she'd rather stand in the rain.

¢¢¢

Carlos met up with his boss in the employee parking lot behind the store. Tom was standing by his red Suburban with the rear window flipped open.

"He's still in there," Carlos reported. "Taking his time, aisle by aisle."

Nodding, Tom reached through the opening. He pulled out a canvas sack and dropped it to the ground. Inside, aluminum bats shook and knocked together – like wind chimes on a front porch.

"I want you to take this to the backroom," he said. "Wait for me by the baler. Keep everybody out. Make sure nobody's around."

Carlos chuckled. "Tom, it happened ten years ago. Darby was in elementary school. He's moved on, everybody has. Let's just kick the guy out and tell him never to come back."

Tom had expected this of his grocery manager. Carlos hated confrontations, avoided them at all costs. It's what kept him from getting promoted. Too soft, everyone had said.

Too numb.

Tom checked his watch. "We don't have much time. Freight load will be here any minute and we need product on the floor. We're out of sugar, the juice aisle's shot, the dairy section could use some attention… We'll manage okay if we don't shuffle our feet."

"You're fucking crazy," Carlos said.

"And you're a goddamn jellyfish," Tom shot back. "Now pick up the bats and wait for me by the baler."

He flipped closed the back window and hit the lock button. "Beat Sunset" was pasted against the glass.

Carlos reached for the green canvas sack, but then let go when a car honked nearby. He looked over, seeing nothing unusual, then back at the bag on the ground. It was an old army duffel with a shoulder strap clipped to both ends. The store's name and phone number were written in black marker across the middle.

The midmorning sun had broken above the trees and the main parking lot wasn't very full. The usual lunch crowd hadn't appeared yet, and not for another twenty minutes.

Tom picked up the bag and the aluminum bats shifted. "We don't have much time," the old store director said to Carlos. "Hurry up and take these. Be a grocery man for once."

¢¢¢

Darby led Shelly over to the couch, sat down and put an arm over her shoulders. She was giving quite a performance, doing her best to sound believable, fake crying into both hands.

"I used to watch you play," Darby said. "All the way up to the end you were the best player on the team. Better than Traci, better than everybody. And I'm not just saying this to make you feel better."

Shelly wiped at her eyes, stared at the floor. It

was the first time she had ever sat on the couch and she hated every bit of the experience. The cushions were flat and the weakened springs made leaning forward difficult. She had to get up.

"Have you ever been up on the roof?" she said, her own eyes brightening at the sudden thought. "You can see everything up there. You could probably see where you live. C'mon, I can show you."

She grabbed Darby's arm and pulled him toward the generator room. He tried fighting it at first, but she proved much stronger than he was.

"I'm already late getting back. Erin will kill me if I don't check in with her."

"Don't worry about Erin. Erin's a teddy bear. All you have to do is ask her about her kids. She'll turn on you faster than a boomerang. C'mon!"

The generator room hummed so loud that you had to scream to be heard. Panels and panels of switches and circuit breakers lined the walls and refrigeration systems. In the corner of the room was a steel ladder suspended from a closed hatch in the ceiling. Shelly climbed up to the combination lock and spun the dial.

"Me and Traci used to go up here all the time," she shouted down to Darby. "Up here we would throw the ball and practice field drills."

She popped the lock and pushed open the square door. Sunlight streamed down as she pulled herself up onto the roof.

Darby followed her up the ladder and peeked his head through the open hatch. The bright sun had his eyes squinting in every direction.

The store's flattop roof was bigger than he'd imagined. "You really could play softball up here." He climbed to his feet, gently bouncing, testing the tarred floor.

Shelly cracked a smile. "Actually, we weren't playing softball. We were taking nitrous hits off of whipped-cream bottles. But don't tell Tom that."

Darby smiled, went over to the roof's edge and peered down at the colorful cars and ant-sized customers in the parking lot. This made him laugh. Across the street was the softball field that Shelly once played on with her old team, a cluster of bright red jerseys practicing in the infield.

"Tomorrow night's the big game," he said. "Are you going?"

Shelly was doing windmill exercises with her arms. "I'll be there. Soon as I get off work."

From an outdoor speaker the intercom bell rang, and Darby leaned forward to listen. It was Erin calling him for a carry-out.

"Shoot, that's me." He raced across the roof and grabbed the ladder's top handle. "I gotta go."

"You can't," Shelly blurted out. On impulse she reached down and put her hand over Darby's. The direct contact startled them both.

"Not yet," she said. "I brought you up here for

another reason." Another reason? What reason? Think fast, Shelly. Think, think…

"Did Traci ever tell you anything?" she said.

"Traci? Like what?"

"You know…" She smiled. "Stuff."

"Stuff?" He looked down at her hand which was still on his, and started thinking certain things, certain *stuff*.

The intercom bell sounded again, but this time the voice, belonging to Tom, called for Shelly to answer. She let go of Darby's hand and slipped on by, down the ladder to the receiver hanging on the break room wall.

"Tom?" she said.

"Shelly," he said back.

"Has he left? Is he gone? I can't keep Darby up here much longer. Erin keeps calling him every five seconds, you gotta tell her to stop."

"Shelly, listen." Tom's voice was calm but stern. "I need you to call the police. I need you to tell them we've caught a shoplifter who isn't cooperating. You hear me? We've caught a shoplifter who isn't cooperating. Tell them to hurry, and to send an ambulance. But make sure they know it's his request, not ours. We're not asking for medical assistance, he is."

¢¢¢

 I heard bits and pieces of the story when I arrived at work later in the afternoon. Shelly told me everything she knew, while Carlos, in confidence, told only parts. He had a cut beneath his left eye and a bandage around his wrist. When I asked him how he got those injuries, his jaw tightened and he clammed up; he grabbed his jacket and went home early without saying another word.
 I hardly saw Darby at the store anymore. His new morning shift had him out the door before I'd clock in. Tom said the change was necessary since he couldn't find anyone else to fill the opening courtesy clerk position. To Darby, who was living on his own and constantly scrounging for money, he didn't have much of a choice. The jump in his hourly wage meant he wouldn't have to find a second job. All he had to do was drop out of school.
 The following night was the big game against Sunset. Business always slowed once the game got underway, and the backroom was a mess. I spent most of the night reorganizing pallets of overstock along the bay wall.
 Darby dropped by the store a little past eight. He pushed through the swinging black doors and stepped into the backroom, wearing a striped collared shirt, dark blue jeans and a silver belt buckle with a bronzed buffalo head. His fake lizard-skinned

cowboy boots were buffed to a shine.

"Look at you all dressed up," I said. "Did you go out to dinner or something?"

Darby didn't answer; he bundled up a piece of plastic wrap lying on the floor and took it to the trashcan. Then he hopped up on a pallet of generic soda and practiced striking a cigarette lighter across his pant leg.

"You should be over at the game," I said.

"Is Shelly still here?"

"She just left a few minutes ago."

Darby snapped the lid closed, snuffing the flame, and put the silver lighter back in his pocket. It wasn't a bad idea. A strong whiff of his aftershave had me wondering if he was flammable.

His mood struck me as different than usual, more contemplative. He leaned forward on the half-cases and clasped his hands. "I talked to an army recruiter today. Nice guy. He pulled me aside and gave me his business card. He liked my work ethic. He said I have hustle."

I pushed a pallet jack under a load of apple juice and pumped the handle. "Don't listen to him," I said. "They're always in here looking for fresh blood."

I swung the apple juice into an open bay, then wheeled the jack across the room to a mixed pallet of canned beans, ramen noodles, salad dressings, and granola bars. Case by case I sorted through the boxes, arranging them first by category, then by flavor, so that everything would be neatly stacked and easy to find. But there was a problem...

"This isn't working," I realized, looking around at the extra product strewn about the floor. "I think I need another pallet."

Next to the receiving office was the loading dock door. I rolled open the gate, secured the chain, then followed Darby through the long plastic flaps hanging from the ceiling.

It was a cool and clear night, perfect conditions for a ballgame. Through a row of tall trees you could see the infield glowing across the street. Sometimes, if you waited long enough, you could hear the ping of an aluminum bat followed by a roaring crowd. A good hit or a great catch would always get the drummers drumming.

"Did you know," Darby said, "that the military purposefully designs its bullets not to kill the enemy but to injure them? You wanna know why?"

On the ledge I stood motionless, waiting, listening, but all I could hear was the faint rumble of cars driving up and down Watson Road.

"Think about it," he said. "You shoot one guy but you don't kill him. Now two of their soldiers have to drop their own guns to rescue their buddy who's hurt. You just eliminated three guns with a single shot. Isn't that genius?"

Darby didn't wait for an answer; he pulled down a wooden pallet from a stack against the wall. By the time I turned around he had gone back inside. In front of me the plastic flaps were swaying with bits of fluorescent light shining through.